"You're a compassionate man."

"It's not compassion, it's faith."

She pushed at her salad with the tines of her fork. "I had that once. That connection that let me see things, understand things like this. But it's gone now."

Now there was anger and outrage and confusion and emptiness. So much emptiness.

"It's not gone. Faith is a choice you make." Paul signaled the waitress for more tea.

A choice she didn't dare make.

She didn't dare try to fill the empty places. It hurt too much to fill them and watch them empty and disappear. People, possessions, emotions—no matter how much you tried to protect them and yourself, you couldn't do it.

You couldn't, and then you had to suffer the loss and failure. She'd suffered enough of both. She had nothing more to give or to lose.

VICKI HINZE

is an award-winning author of nearly thirty novels, four nonfiction books and hundreds of articles published in as many as sixty-three countries. She lives in Florida with her husband, near her children and grands, and she gets cranky if she must miss one of their ball games. Vicki loves to visit with readers and invites you to join her at vickihinze.com or on Facebook at Facebook.com/vicki.hinze.author.

SURVIVE
THE
NIGHT

VICKI HINZE

Love Inspired

Recycling programs
for this product may
not exist in your area.

™ LOVE INSPIRED BOOKS

ISBN-13: 978-0-373-44509-7

SURVIVE THE NIGHT

www.LoveInspiredBooks.com

Printed in U.S.A.

"I know the plans I have for you," declares the Lord,
"plans to prosper you and not to harm you,
plans to give you hope and a future."
—*Jeremiah* 29:11

In honor of Kathy Carmichael

We are gifted with friends to share our joys and troubles. Thank you for being my friend, Kathy, and for the blessing of being your Sister of the Heart.

ONE

"Tired?"

Della Jackson latched her seat belt, then looked over at Paul Mason, driving his SUV. Her day had started just after five. It was now nineteen hours long, but she had to give credit to her boss, Madison McKay, owner of Lost, Inc. Holding an "open house" at the small private investigating firm where Della had worked since returning to Florida three years ago was a brilliant idea. Holding it during North Bay's annual street festival was beyond brilliant and now a proven, resounding success.

"I passed tired about nine o'clock. Not that your company hasn't been great." On a horse wearing a cowboy hat or in a black tux as he was now, Paul Mason was gorgeous and charming. Black hair, gray eyes and lean and fit with a face chiseled by a loving hand. More importantly to Della, he was a man of character, trusted, and he expected nothing from her. That made him the perfect nondate date for any event but especially for one of Madison's formal soirees, which Della never attended without a direct command-performance memo.

Paul's arm draped the steering wheel. "Can I say something without you going postal on me?"

Odd remark. "Sure." In their three years of being close friends, hadn't they always spoken freely? From the first time she'd talked to him on the phone from Tennessee through his organization, Florida Vet Net, and he'd agreed to help her relocate to Florida, she thought they had done nothing but speak freely.

He braked for a group of about thirty festivalgoers to cross the street. One boy about twelve had the Seminole emblem painted on his cheek: Red is good.

Her dress. So he had noticed that she always wore black. Was he like her landlady's granddaughter next door? Gracie, a precocious eight-year-old, had taken one look at the red dress her grandmother was rehemming because Della had hemmed the silk with dental floss and asked if Della was done mourning.

What mother ever stopped mourning the death of a child? What woman stopped mourning the resulting breakup of her marriage? "The black dress didn't fit."

Disappointment flashed through Paul's eyes. "Ah, I see." He turned onto Highway 20, then minutes later, south into her subdivision. "You seemed to have fun tonight."

"You know I did." They'd danced, enjoyed a battle of the bands and had a grand time. Fun. She'd had fun.

The thought sank in, and a flood of guilt swarmed in right behind it.

He clicked on his blinker to turn onto her street. "It's okay for you to have fun, Della. And to wear clothes that aren't black. It's been three years."

"I know." She'd heard it all from everyone—her former pastor, her landlady, her boss, her boss's assistant—and now from Paul.

"But knowing it and feeling it are two different things?" he suggested.

He understood. Paul always understood. "Exactly." Days passing on a calendar didn't change the grief or loss in a mother's heart. That was the part the others didn't seem to understand. The ache and emptiness were still fresh, the wounds still raw. She sighed, glanced out the window. Gracie stood on Della's front porch. What was that she was holding? "But I am working on— *Stop!*"

Paul hit the brakes hard, screeched to a stop. "What's wrong?"

Della didn't pause to answer but grabbed the door, flung it open and scrambled out. "Gracie!" she screamed, her voice frantic, and ran full out toward her cottage. *Oh, please no. Don't let it happen again.* "Put down that package!"

Gracie stood statue-still, her eyes stretched wide, like a terrified deer blinded by headlights.

"Put the box down, Gracie." Della softened her voice. "Do it now. Right now."

Gracie set the box on the porch's floor and then just stood beside it.

Della snatched her off the porch, buried her against her hammering chest and ran across the postage-stamp-sized yard to the sidewalk near the street, putting the most distance possible between the package and the child, using her own body as a shield.

Paul ran up to them. "What's wrong?"

Della ignored him. "Gracie, didn't your gran tell you not to get my mail?"

"I—I didn't, Della," she said on a stuttered breath. "You're squishing me."

Della loosened her hold. "Where did you get the box?"

"It wasn't in the mailbox, I promise. It was on the porch by the swing." Her voice cracked. "I was scared you wouldn't see it and—"

Della's heart still banged against her ribs, threatened to thump out of her chest. She was shaking. Hard. "I appreciate it, but next time you listen to me. Don't get my mail anymore or any packages. Got it?"

A fat tear rolled down Gracie's cheek.

Paul smiled and flicked away Gracie's tear. "Della knows

you were trying to help, and she's sorry she sounds so angry. She's not, you know."

"She sounds plenty mad." Gracie's chin quivered.

"No, I'm not mad." Della felt like a slug. A terrified slug, but still a slug. "I was scared."

"Why?" Gracie and Paul asked simultaneously.

Oh, boy. She was in for it now, but it was past time for the truth. "Gracie, you know what happened to Danny, right?" Just speaking her son's name hurt, reopened the gaping wounds in her battered heart.

Gracie nodded. Light from the streetlamp had the glittery face paint from the festival sparkling on her cheeks. "His daddy was holding him and he opened the mailbox and it exploded. His daddy got hurt, but Danny went to heaven. Now he lives with your mom and dad and my grandpa."

"That's right." Della said it, and would give her eyeteeth to still believe it. But her beliefs or lack of them were her problem, not Gracie's. "This is my fault. I didn't want to frighten you, but I should have told you I'm worried the man who did that to Danny might do it again. That's why I don't want you getting my mail and why I sounded so angry. When I saw you on the porch with that box…I was really scared."

Gracie curled her arms around Della's neck and hugged her fiercely. Her breath warmed Della's neck, melted the icy chill steeped in her bones. "I'm not going to heaven yet. It'll be a long, long time. Gran said."

Gran was the ultimate authority on all things. "That's good to know." Della blew out a steadying breath, then set Gracie down on the sidewalk. "You run on home now. It's late and your gran is waiting." What was Miss Addie thinking, letting Gracie come outside this late at night alone?

"She doesn't know I'm gone. She's in the shower."

That explained that. "What made you come out here?" Della should have asked that before now, and probably would have, if seeing the child holding that package hadn't scared ten years off her life.

"I saw the man put the box on the porch."

A chill streaked through Della. "Did you know him?"

She shook her head. "It was too dark. I just saw the box moving. He was carrying it."

"He was wearing dark clothes, then?" Della asked.

"I dunno. I only saw the box until he left. Then when he got to the sidewalk I saw him."

Because of the streetlight. "Would you know him again?"

"No. Everything was black." She tilted her head. "Well, except his shoes."

"Did you see his face?"

"No."

Paul spoke softly. "Gracie, are you sure it was a man?"

"I dunno. He was bigger than Della, but not as big as you. I couldn't see."

"Okay, honey," Della said. "You go on home now before your gran can't find you and gets scared."

"Yes, ma'am."

"And no more leaving the house without her knowing it," Paul said.

"Yes, sir." Gracie cut across the grass and headed next door. "Night, Della. Bye, Mr. Mason."

"Good night, Gracie."

"I wish she'd seen more," Paul said.

"I hope he didn't see her." Della's gaze collided with Paul's. "You're not thinking it was FedEx, are you?"

"At midnight?" She muffled a grunt. "No."

"Neither am I," he said, then waited, clearly expecting her to explain her behavior and her concerns.

Della hesitated, staring back at the porch at the box, but Paul let the silence between them stretch, blatantly waiting for her to look at him. Resigned, she did. At least he wasn't scowling.

"Spill it."

"Spill what?" The porch light cast streaks of light across the sidewalk, but it wasn't so dark she didn't see the stern look in his eyes. She could try to act as if everything was fine now that Gracie was safely tucked into her own cottage, pretend that her being outside was what really terrified Della and hope he'd go home so she could examine the box on her own, but that required deceit. She hated deceit and she'd never practiced it with Paul. The idea of doing so now grated on her. Just considering it made her feel slimy.

"Don't minimize this." He frowned. "Your explanation satisfied Gracie, but I know you, Della Jackson. You're not suddenly scared of another mailbox bomb. Not with Dawson locked away in a mental hospital. So what's going on?"

He knew her too well. "Dawson isn't in the mental hospital anymore. He's out."

Surprised lit across Paul's face. "Since when?"

"Apparently, for about six weeks—"

"And you didn't tell me?"

"There's no need to shout at me. My hearing is just fine." She frowned up at him. "I just found out two weeks ago."

"A month after the fact? But they were supposed to give you advance notice."

"Yes, they were, but they didn't. I fell through the crack."

"So two weeks ago, they notified you and you didn't think it was significant enough to mention?"

"I was going to tell you. I just hadn't gotten around to it yet. My caseload has been a bear, and then there was the open house—it's just been kind of crazy."

"You're still making excuses. Please don't." She opened her mouth, but he lifted a finger. "You figure Dawson is out and knows where you are because…?"

She clamped her jaw and stared at the box on the porch. Anything she said would upset Paul more and she didn't want to do that.

"Della, I know something has happened. Just Dawson's

release wouldn't put you in the panic you were in when you saw Gracie. Stop making me pull teeth, woman, and tell me what's going on."

"The truth is, I'm not sure yet." She summoned her courage and headed toward the box.

From the edge of the porch, she studied the label and felt the blood drain from her face. "But we need to call the police."

He walked over to where she stood. "Why?"

"Because—" she spared him a glance "—it says it's from Tennessee."

His frown faded and his face brightened. "Maybe Jeff's finally sent you the pictures of Danny."

She'd asked her ex for a photo of her son every month for three years and had gotten nothing. No photo, no response whatsoever. "Highly doubtful—no." She more closely examined the box. "This isn't from Jeff, and I don't know anyone else in Tennessee anymore."

"How do you know it's not from him? If there's no one else—"

Having the benefit of insights he did not, she pointed but didn't touch the package. "See this code on the shipping label?"

Paul read it and then looked over at her, his expression grave. "It's a Florida zip code."

"Walton County." Della nodded. "But someone clearly wanted me to think the box was from Tennessee." The return address had been written in black marker.

"That's more than enough for me." Paul pulled out his cell and dialed.

"Who are you calling?" Della asked.

Paul lifted a wait-a-second finger. "Major Beech, it's Paul Mason. Fine. Yeah, a good turnout." He moved to put himself between the box and Della. "I've got a suspicious package over at Della Jackson's cottage."

Major Harrison Beech. Why was Paul calling the base and not the local police? Della grimaced. "It could be nothing."

She said it, but it didn't feel like nothing. It felt like a huge something.

"Thanks, Beech." Paul hung up and guided Della away from the package. "He's coming out with some friends."

A team of professionals. His hand on her arm was firm, leading her back toward the sidewalk. "Why did you call him?"

"He's an explosives specialist."

"But we don't know that there are explosives in the box, Paul."

"Which is why it's best to be prudent." He stopped. "We do know the package was delivered under suspicious circumstances."

"But Beech?" The military reminded her of her active duty days when she'd been stationed at the base here, and of all she'd lost while serving in Afghanistan. Things she'd worked hard to forget but failed, and now worked hard to accept. "Couldn't the police handle it?" Actually, she didn't want them called, either. She didn't need the police.

Now that she'd absorbed the shock of seeing Gracie on the porch holding that box, she wanted to check it out herself. It could be a prank, related to one of her cases. Could be a practical joke of some sort, or anything other than something dangerous. She was a professional investigator, for pity's sake. If the local police considered her a hysterical woman, her professional effectiveness would be hampered on every case she worked from now on.

Yet Paul's reason for calling Major Beech intrigued her. Why had he done that? Oh, she'd heard what he'd said. But she knew him, and his reasons would never be that simple. There was definitely more to it.

"The local police are not explosives specialists, and they're tied up with the festival. They'd have to get a unit from Walton County to come in and, frankly, Walton would probably just call the base for assistance anyway. Calling Beech direct saves time." Paul led her down the sidewalk toward his SUV. "Let's wait in the car."

All true, but still not everything. What more was there? "You've got a bad feeling about this, don't you?" Della sensed it in him, just as she felt it in the pit of her stomach. Maybe it was their military training. Paul had served in special operations. Della had served in the intelligence realm as a computer specialist. Both positions required skill sets that included honed instincts.

Or maybe it wasn't their common military experience but the personal bond connecting them that put them on a kindred wavelength. Whatever the reason, they both had a feeling about this, and it wasn't good.

"Yeah, I do, Della." He wrapped a protective arm around her shoulder. "A real bad feeling."

She shivered and he pulled her closer.

Crouching low, he hid in the darkness between two fat bushes and watched them walk to the black SUV and get inside. He'd chosen this spot across the street because it was void of light; she'd never spot him, yet he could see every move she made.

Why didn't you just open the box? Frustrated, he cast an agitated glare at her neighbor's house, the cottage next door. It was that stupid kid's fault. If she hadn't interfered, Della would have found the package. He'd have seen her open it. There's no way she would have walked away without opening it. He'd have seen her panic and felt her fear.

He thrived on her fear.

For six weeks, the anticipation had been building, clawing at his stomach, urging him to rush. Temptation burned so strong but he'd strained mightily against it and fortunately his leash had held—at least, thus far. *Discipline, man. To win requires discipline.*

It did. Enormous discipline. Della Jackson was not a fool.

Yet neither was he. Each step had to be weighed, considered, calculated, the consequences determined from all sides. He'd planned down to the minutest detail. Created a backup contingency plan. Monitored and measured each act, each response, every possible reaction, and it was a good thing he had.

She'd picked up on him following her right away—amazingly fast, actually. He begrudgingly gave her props for that. The woman had skills and the instincts to make her as good an investigator as she had been with computers. Those instincts made her dangerous.

But his instincts and skills were stronger, more seasoned, perfected over two decades in a series of trials by fire. Soon she'd discover just how much superiority that gave him. Soon he'd see—

Three cars whipped around the corner and slid to a stop at the curb in front of her cottage.

So they weren't cutting and running. Mason had stuck in his nose and called for backup. No cops. Military backup. A shudder rippled through his body, pressed his stomach into the cool dirt. *Well, well.* Interesting if mildly disappointing yet not wholly unexpected. He could deal with it. So he wouldn't get to see her face when she saw what was inside the box. He could imagine her reaction easily enough.

Horror and then rage. Helpless and hopeless and then finally, finally...Della Jackson eaten alive with fear.

Inescapable, merciless, unrelenting fear.

He could wait. Not tonight, but before this was done he would see all those things in her and more. And when she was emotionally drained dry and wrung out with nothing left and too weak to run, then...

Then?

Then he would kill her.

Turning away, he slipped into the night.

"Della. Paul." Major Harrison Beech extended his hand. "Good to see you, though I'm sorry about the circumstance."

He was a big man with close-cropped hair and a bulky build dressed in his BDU—battle dress uniform. The camo was light, but most of it was now, since they'd been at war in the desert for a decade. "I'm not sure what the circumstances are," Della said honestly. "I hope we haven't troubled you for nothing."

Beech motioned to his men to retrieve the box from the porch. "I hope you have." He spared her a smile, grabbing a gear bag from his vehicle. "Any reason to expect explosives?"

"We haven't examined the package," Paul said. "But Della was the target of a mailbox bomb when she was active duty."

"Yes." Sadness crossed his face. "You were in theater, Afghanistan, but your husband and son…"

She nodded. Clearly he'd been briefed on her dossier on his way over. "The man who did it, Leo Dawson, wasn't convicted. He was a mental patient they'd cut loose. So they sent him back."

"Let me guess. He's out now."

Again she nodded. "About six weeks, though I just learned of it. But I'm not sure this package is from him. That incident happened over three years ago. He has nothing to connect me to North Bay."

"As I recall, you weren't stationed here when he planted the bomb."

"No, I'd already left the base." When here, she had officially been assigned to Personnel, but actually she'd been in a top-secret facility only those with extremely high clearances knew existed. They referred to it as the Nest. Her mission had been to protect the Nest's computer assets. Not that she knew the facility's purpose. Only the commander and vice commander had clearance for that tight need-to-know loop. "When my family was attacked, I was stationed in Tennessee but deployed to Afghanistan." She crossed her arms. Talking about this dredged up all the old feelings, painful memories she didn't want to relive.

Two of his men methodically tested the package. Della glanced back to Paul.

"There's a discrepancy between the return address and the actual shipping label," Paul told Beech. "One's Tennessee, the other a Walton County zip code." Waloka's neighboring county to the east.

"Any credible suspects besides the mental patient?" Beech asked.

"Dozens," she confessed. "Working my cases for Lost, Inc., I ruffle a few feathers."

Paul smiled. "Della's persistent about finding people who are lost—even those who don't want to be found. Makes for some grateful friends, but for a few annoyed enemies, too." He hiked a thumb toward the front door. "I'm going to check things out inside while you're here."

Beech nodded and Paul went into the cottage, leaving the door open.

Beech kept one eye on it and one on her. "You work for Madison McKay. Persistence runs through her whole agency."

"I do, and it does." Persistence flowed through every staff member's veins.

He crossed his arms. "Any enemies in recent memory stand out from the rest?"

"No." She'd reviewed all the cases she'd handled in the past six months, and the mess in her office showed it. Missing husbands, kids seeking birth mothers, runaway teens, the odd embezzler and witness. But after running updates on old and new cases, she hadn't seen anyone with serious potential for doing something to her like this.

A few minutes later, Paul returned.

"Anything?" Beech asked him.

"Nothing at all."

"Major Beech," one of his men called out. "Package is clear. Permission to open it, sir?"

"Granted." He turned back to Della. "Why did you call me?"

"I didn't. Paul did." She shrugged. "I would have checked it out myself." He gave her a strange look, so she explained. "I've had military explosives training."

"I see." That apparently hadn't been relayed from her dossier, or he hadn't had access to the entire thing. He glanced at Paul for further explanation. "So you called me because…"

"She's been separated from the military for over three years. A lot's changed." His words and expression were at odds.

Beech pursed his lips, nodding. "And you thought I'd keep the chain of evidence intact and my mouth shut about this."

"That, too." Paul smiled.

"Understood—provided we find nothing that poses a security risk."

"Fair enough."

"Major, you'll want to see this." The man stood bent, shining a high-intensity flashlight into the box.

Beech double-timed it over to where they stood. Della and Paul followed.

"Hardly benevolent." Beech motioned to her to look.

Della peered inside. A bloody knife lay on a bed of shredded newspaper. She sucked in a sharp breath, forced herself to not back away.

"There's a note," one of Beech's men said.

Signaling with a lift of his chin, Beech issued an order. "Extract it."

Another of his men pulled out a test pack, prepared a smear slide and then ran some preliminary studies on blood he'd gotten from the knife. "Tracking human, sir."

Della swallowed hard. She felt Paul looking at her but lacked the courage to meet his gaze.

"Read the note," Beech told the first.

"Yes, sir." He held the paper tilted to the light.

Della clasped her hands at her sides and stiffened, bracing.

The man cleared his throat, then read, "'Your time is coming, Della. Once in a while, could you eat something other

than Chinese food? Who will clean all those cartons out of
your fridge after you're gone? I wonder, but soon I'll know.'
It's signed, 'D.B.D.'"

Della sucked in a sharp breath, absorbed the shock.

TWO

The color drained from Paul's face. "He's been in her house. In her refrigerator."

Beech looked at Della. "Who's D.B.D.?"

"I don't know." She swung her gaze to Paul. "I'm not being evasive, I really don't know."

"Who else has a key?"

She looked back at Beech. "No one. Well, Miss Addie, next door. She's my landlord. But I haven't given a key to anybody."

Paul asked, "Do you have one stashed outside somewhere in case you lock yourself out?"

"No." Her mouth went dry, her inner lips sticking to her teeth. "I never thought to do that."

"What about the Chinese food?"

"I ordered a ton of it Thursday night. I couldn't decide what I wanted, so I got a little bit of everything."

"So there are a lot of Chinese food cartons in your fridge and they weren't there before Thursday?"

"That's right." Della frowned.

"That narrows down the timeline on when he entered."

It did.

A muscle in Paul's jaw ticked. "You're not telling me everything."

She wasn't, and she didn't want to now. Not with Beech here. "I can't tell you what I don't know."

"No explosives, so it's your call," Beech said. "What do you want to do?"

What was she going to do? He'd been in her home.... The threats were definitely escalating. "The only person in Tennessee I know is my ex. I'd like to check his status."

"You two still close?"

"No. But I can't look his way without evidence." She'd been on the receiving end of that from him. She'd never deliberately put another person through that. "I need to track this package."

"What about the knife?" Beech asked. "Don't you want the locals to take it from us to protect the chain of evidence?"

She wanted this mess to go away. She wanted peace. She'd never have it, but the shade of it she'd spent three years building was as close as she'd get, and she wanted it back. "Can you keep possession and give me a little time to see what I can find out?"

"I can." Beech rubbed at his thick neck. "I shouldn't, but I will."

Della knew why he was willing. When she'd been assigned at the Nest, Beech had been at the Pentagon. According to Madison's assistant, Mrs. Renault, he'd hooked up with an ambassador's assistant named Christina. They'd been discovered, she'd been fired and he'd been sent to Iceland for a year. They'd done nothing wrong, but he'd played by the rules and been burned—and that's why Paul had called him. Beech would understand. Others wouldn't. Beech had returned from Iceland and married Christina, so at least things had worked out for him. But he hadn't forgotten the challenges of having suspicion hanging over his head. "I appreciate it, Major."

Beech nodded, turning to one of the guys. "Log it in. I want art, and cut her a written receipt for it."

Art. Every conceivable kind of photo of everything.

"Yes, sir." He began taking snapshots of the outside of the box and working his way to capturing images of the contents.

"Could you email me a photo of the shipping label?" Della asked.

"Yes, ma'am." He nodded and got busy.

Soon they were done and departing. "Della," Major Beech said. "You realize you're on dangerous ground, right? If this was Dawson, he's crazy and he has a violent history. If not, whoever it was has been in your home. Don't take that lightly."

"I'm not, and I am aware." *Very dangerous ground.* She'd been acutely aware of danger for weeks.

"Very well. If you need me, call. Paul has the number."

"Thank you." Della shook his hand and watched them load into their vehicles and pull away as silently and swiftly as they'd arrived.

She turned to Paul, whose expression was more sober than she ever recalled seeing it. "What?"

"What?" He frowned. "Della, what's going on? You're surprised but not shocked. Someone has invaded your home and you're not acting violated. Why?"

"I feel violated—everything victims usually feel. I'm just trying to keep my wits."

His frown warned he wasn't buying it for a second. "I brought you to North Bay. I got you in with Lost, Inc. If some nut on one of your cases is after you, I have to help. We're friends, and that's what friends do. Just don't hold out on me, Della. Tell me the truth."

"I really don't know who he is or if it's personal or case-connected. But this isn't first contact. It started with me sensing someone was following me." The hair on her neck had stood on end. Her flesh had crept and crawled. Her every instinct had shouted with certainty that someone was watching her, but she hadn't seen anyone. Still, she knew. She knew.

"And then…?"

"I got the first note."

"The *first* note?" Surprise rippled through his voice, charged the air between them. "How many notes have there been?"

Survive the Night

"This is the second one." Her stomach knotted.

"What was in the first package?"

"It wasn't a package. Just the note. I was leaving for work one morning and found it under the windshield wiper on my car."

"So this person already knew where you lived and had been in your garage?"

"Yes and no. He knew where I lived, but the car was parked outside that night, not in the garage." She risked a glance up at Paul. "Baby killer—that's all the first note said." The words hurt her throat. Made her eyes sting.

"What?" Paul looked thunderstruck.

No way could she say it twice. She'd been honest but glossed over details of what had happened in Tennessee. Now she had no choice but to be specific. "Leo Dawson used that same term." The urge to cry bit her hard. She refused it, just as she'd refused to shed the first tear since hearing about Danny. "Before I was deployed, Dawson and I got into an argument in my driveway. I was in uniform, out getting my newspaper. Dawson lived a few houses down the street. He'd heard I was being deployed and he blindsided me and beat me half to death. He said I had no right to abandon my son to go to Afghanistan. Then he called me…that. I don't for sure know why. The man's crazy. Nobody knew why."

"How old was Dawson?"

"Fifty-five or so."

"Vietnam era," Paul said. "Many called soldiers 'baby killer'—it was a common antiwar slur."

"That's what his psychiatrist said. Dawson had mental challenges, and events just made them worse. Around the neighborhood, people said he often slipped in and out of that era. His doctor said there were also people who exploited him. Apparently after the war he had been different but functional. They thought he was safe to cut loose, so they did. From all accounts, he did well until 9/11 happened. I guess the trauma of it and the war that followed set him off again. That was what his doctor suspected, anyway. To him, anyone with a weapon of any kind was a baby killer. That's how his twisted mind associated things."

"What did you suspect?" Paul asked.

"Nothing more than that until the mailbox bomb. But the day he assaulted me in the driveway, he told the police a mother should never leave her child, especially not to fight in a war. That a mother didn't belong in the military, and one who was and would leave didn't deserve a child." She blinked hard, swallowed a knot from her throat. "He was clearly unbalanced. The police arrested him, and the D.A. settled. Dawson went back to the mental hospital and the D.A. didn't pursue a conviction for the assault." She shrugged. "I'm not blaming anyone. It seemed right at the time to me, too. He was sick. None of us could have known Dawson would get out and do what he did to Danny and Jeff." Danny had died and Jeff had been injured. He swore he'd rather have died, too, and having felt that way herself, Della felt certain he'd been sincere.

"So Dawson is loose and you suspect he's stalking you?"

"I suspect it, but I don't know it. I haven't located him. I checked with some of our former associates." Paul would intuit that she meant people still active in the intelligence community. She and Paul had revealed working in the realm during their assignments, but they hadn't discussed specifics. Often she'd wondered if he'd been assigned to the Nest, too, and, if so, in what capacity. But of course she hadn't asked. One of the first things you learned was to not ask questions if you didn't want to be asked questions you didn't want to answer. "They've confirmed Dawson's release and that he returned home, but then he disappeared. No sightings for the last ten days."

"So he could be here."

"Or anywhere else in the world." In ten days, he could have traveled to Fiji or Siberia. But in her gut she knew he hadn't.

He was here. He had to be here. Who else would send her a bloody knife and threatening notes?

"I know you've checked. Nothing on travel, credit cards, any of the usual?"

She shook her head. "Nothing."

"What about comparing his handwriting to the first note?"

"Zero cooperation on that. Can't invade his privacy without formal charges."

"Which you haven't sought because you lack sufficient proof."

"Exactly." The local police would tar and feather her. They had clashed a few times on her cases, often enough for her to know not to expect any cooperation much less any favors. That was her fault. Too often, she pushed the line. She never crossed it, but she straddled it whenever the situation warranted. The police didn't much appreciate that. If she stood on their side of the fence, she wouldn't appreciate it, either.

"We can have a comparison done on the two notes—you still have the first one, right?"

"Oh, yeah."

"Did he sign it the same way as this one—D.B.D.?"

"No, he didn't." Della hedged. Paul wouldn't like this. "But I think it's the same person."

"Why?" He lifted a finger. "No, wait. Let me save us some time and ask the right question. How did he sign the first note?"

She forced herself to meet Paul's gaze. "Dead by Dawn."

Paul pulled out his phone and started to key in a number.

"Stop," Della insisted, covering his phone with her hand. "Who are you calling?"

"We need help, Della." Paul frowned but didn't touch the keys. "If we can't prove this incident is case-connected and you can't draw a connection from Dawson to you, then we're dealing with an unknown. We need access and resources—and more eyes to keep you safe."

"I know you're not calling the Office of Special Investigations."

In situations where ex-intelligence officers were under threat, that was the protocol, but they'd checked that box, if only unofficially, by his calling Beech. The last thing Della needed was the OSI digging into this. They would proceed as if she'd done something military-related that she shouldn't have done, until it was proven otherwise. They both knew the drill. They'd worked it, and they understood the necessity for it, but it could put Della in a bad position with the military and hamper her in finding the stalker.

Paul stared at her through the shadowy light cast from the front porch. "We should call them, the local police and the FBI."

Yes, former military members embedded in intelligence positions with their level of clearances were required to report all threats of any kind to the OSI, not to civilian authorities. But he had said all of them—OSI, local and FBI. She had to be wondering why.

"I don't understand the FBI." She kept her hand on his phone. "But please don't do that to me."

"You don't understand—"

"I understand plenty." Heat crept into her voice. "The OSI has been watching me like a hawk since I got the news about Danny's death. You know I was a mess. Depression, grief—all that. I worked Intel, Paul. I know too much about too many things, and you know they don't trust anyone who knows anything and is emotionally stressed. You call them, and the first thing they're going to do is declare me a security risk. They'll get my Class-C license revoked. Without it, I can't do my job as an investigator, not to mention my carry permit. That happens, and if this stalker does try to kill me, I won't even be able to defend myself."

"Della, listen to me. Just listen, okay?" Paul paused, clearly hoping she would. "You know my training. You also know my sister."

"What's Maggie got to do with this?"

"I've protected her since we were kids. I've had to. But something happened last year that proved beyond any doubt, when you're dealing with monsters capable of this kind of evil, one man's protection isn't enough. We need help."

Tension crackled off her like hot live wires. "We're not going to any of them," she insisted, then fell silent.

"All right. You've got a point. The OSI would consider you a security risk, and probably would work to yank your license and carry permit until you proved you weren't. But the blood on that knife tested human. Whose blood is it? And this stalker was in your home. He isn't some amateur. He's a serious stalker who could be anybody."

"It has to be Dawson. He used the same words in the note."

"Dawson is a mental patient. He could have told anyone, dozens already know it, and this stalker could be a copycat or someone who's read about Dawson in the paper." Paul winced. At the moment, he would give everything he had—his money, his ranch, even his horses and his beloved rottweiler, Jake— to not have to dispute her. "The fact is, we don't yet know the stalker's identity. This incident could be unrelated to Dawson. It could be related to me. I make a lot of enemies at Vet Net. It could be someone trying to get to me through you."

"Doubtful. You help people reintegrate into civilian life after their military service, rebuild their families and find jobs. Okay, so some get irritated because you're persistent, push-ing for veteran's rights, but they're not the kind of people to inflict physical harm."

"Not always true." He let her see his worry. "You remem-ber the Gary Crawford case?"

"The notorious serial killer. Sure, everyone not living under a rock knows about him."

"Maggie was nearly his victim. The Utah incident last

year—that was him, and he got away. It's possible he's your stalker."

"Why would he come after me?"

"Because you're important to me." Paul clasped her hand. "Della, we can't discount him. He left notes with his victims that he signed *Baby Killer*."

Shock pumped through Della's body. "Maggie was profiling Gary Crawford's case?" She'd been an FBI agent, but she wasn't anymore.

"Yes."

"But she's an artist now." With her off the case he had no reason to hunt down Maggie, much less her brother, and even less reason to come after her brother's friend. "No, it's Dawson. He assaulted me. He bombed my mailbox and killed…"

Paul spared her having to say her son's name. "Are you a hundred percent positive that you weren't Leo Dawson's intended victim?"

She lifted her hands. "I'd been in Afghanistan for months."

"Did he know that?"

Della opened her mouth to answer but stopped short. Had he known? After a stream of home invasions, robberies and property thefts, the military kept specific deployment dates and names quiet to avoid making victims of those left at home. They even ordered soldiers to have their addresses removed from phone books. Dawson could have assumed the assault had kept her from being deployed. He could have believed she was at home and she would open the mailbox. "I don't know."

"So you could have been the intended victim?"

"Maybe." It actually made more sense. Why would someone bomb a mailbox claiming to be protecting a child or use the "baby killer" slur to harm a child? More guilt layered on inside her. Dawson must have thought she was at home and she would be his victim. *Oh, Danny. Mommy is so sorry.* She crossed her chest with her arms to hold in the hurt. "Dawson likely did mean to kill me—" her voice cracked "—and my poor baby just got in the way."

Paul clasped her shoulder. "I don't know, Della. All I'm saying is that we both have enemies. Everyone in North Bay considers us a couple no matter how many times we tell them we're not, so we shouldn't just assume Dawson is your stalker. The reason for this could be tied to me." The expression on Paul's face sobered. "I hope not. But it's possible, and the FBI or the local police could know something we don't."

What Paul hadn't said was as significant as what he had. "You didn't notify the OSI then—when you and Maggie were attacked?"

"Maggie was the target. I was collateral damage, so no. There was no reason to contact them. But that's beside the point. I couldn't protect her alone and—"

"This is why you don't date much," Delia interrupted.

The topic shift seemed to surprise him. "I see who I want when I want."

"But you don't date because you don't want to put anyone else in jeopardy." Finally their relationship made sense. He spent time with Della because they *weren't* dating. She was safe.

Except that, while their relationship had started out that way, now everyone thought they were dating no matter what they said.

So why hadn't he stopped spending so much time with her?

She'd have to think about that. Right now she just wished the idea of them being more than friends didn't thrill her or make her heart flutter and her breath hitch. But it did, and that terrified her.

"Look, all I'm saying is we need help. This is complicated. Until we can prove who the stalker is, we need to keep an open mind. He could be anyone."

"I hear you, but I have to say that this is too much like Dawson for me to really believe it's anyone else."

Paul lifted her hands, pressed them to his cheek. "And I can't dismiss that Gary Crawford could have found out what happened to Danny and is using it to get to me through you. I survived his attack, and he hates loose ends." Fear flashed through Paul's eyes. "I'm afraid—"

"He'll kill me to hurt you," she interjected. "I understand." She slid off the porch step, stood up and then moved away from him so she could think beyond the feel of his work-roughened hands on her face. "Did your guy stalk his victims?"

"Yes." Paul leaned forward, spread his feet and laced his fingers at his knees. "And he's very good." He looked up at her. "Whoever sent this package—Dawson, Crawford, some crazy copycat—he's dangerous and smart. We need help to stop him before he hurts you."

"I'm not opposed to help. I am opposed to going through normal channels for it." Her chest went tight. "You have to understand, Paul." It took all she had to meet his gaze. "I've got so little left. Going through normal channels, I could lose it all and gain nothing."

Anguish crossed his face. "But, Della—"

"No. We need help. I get it. But we're going to get it my way." She took his phone and keyed in her boss's number. "I hate my way, but things are what they are. I have no choice."

He dragged a frustrated hand through his wind-tossed hair. "What is it you hate—exactly?"

"Bringing my dirty laundry to work." Della stared into his eyes, motioning for him to scoot over on the step and make room for her. "Madison, it's Della." She sat down beside him. Sounds of the party flooded in the background. "Can you hear me?"

"Barely. The diehards are still going strong here, as you can tell." Madison laughed, soft and melodic. "Let me get somewhere quiet. Just a sec." A brief pause and then she returned. The background noise faded. "What's up?"

No sense in sugarcoating it. "I'm in trouble and I need your help."

"Can we handle it, or should I summon the troops?"

Paul apparently could hear every word. "Tell her to summon the troops. If this is Crawford, we're going to need all the help we can get."

"I heard him," Madison said. "That's Paul and he said Crawford. As in Gary Crawford?"

"It is, and he did, but we don't know if Crawford is involved. It could be someone else." She'd explain in person.

"Either way, Paul sounds worried."

So, too, did Madison. "He is." Della held Paul's gaze. Beyond worried. *Guilty. Sick inside that maybe he had led Crawford to put a target on her back.* Understanding all too well that displaced guilt felt as real as earned guilt, she clasped his hand.

"I take it he'll be with you, then?"

"He will." It'd take an earthquake or a brick of C-4 explosives to hold him back—if Della wanted to and, honestly speaking, she didn't.

"All right. Be safe on your way in. People are still dancing in the street. The mayor said this is the biggest festival crowd he's seen in thirty years. We'll be waiting for you in the conference room."

"Thanks, Madison." Della ended the call, locked up the cottage and then returned to Paul on the porch.

"You've been crying."

She hadn't been. But walking into her home had put her in a cold sweat. "You know I don't cry anymore."

"But you're upset."

"I am." She rubbed her arms. "Wondering what he touched." She shook. "Everything looks fine, but I still feel as if I need a bath."

"That's normal."

"I know. But I still hate it."

He opened the SUV door. She slid inside, onto the buttery-soft leather seat. "I hope you're wrong. Dawson's bad enough, but he's sick. Crawford is…"

"A monster who likes to kill." Paul's eyes burned with worry, guilt and now regret. "Della, if I've put you on his radar—"

"Don't go there. We don't know, but we are where we are. At least we've got each other." She buckled her safety belt. "Can you get me a dossier on Crawford, just in case?" She honestly didn't believe he was involved. This smacked of Leo Dawson, but it'd make Paul feel better if she weighed in his concerns.

"It's waiting for you. I emailed it while you were locking up the cottage." Paul put the gearshift in Reverse and then backed out of the cottage's driveway.

He was always thoughtful, prepared and protective. Della loved those qualities in him. "When you get yourself a wife, she's going to appreciate many things about you, Paul Mason."

"Yeah, I do good email. That'll impress her."

Della smiled at him. "You do good everything."

"Thank you." His smile broadened. "I believe that's the nicest thing you've ever said to me."

Was it? Really? All he'd done for her, and she'd never offered him kind words? That was pathetic. "I think you're an amazing man. The way you helped get me here and find a job and a place to live."

"That's just part of my job."

So was talking her through the hard times. Being with her on the anniversary no mother should have to acknowledge. "You do it well, and it's a lot more to those who need it." She rubbed his arm "I've seen people you've helped, Paul. They look at you with such respect and admiration."

"They were in a jam. Anyone could have done what I did."

"Could have, but didn't." She stroked back an errant lock of hair from his ear. "You did." A tenderness she didn't want to feel filled her. It startled her. This was Paul. She couldn't have these feelings for Paul. He was her best friend. And one of the first rules of survival was to never risk what you couldn't afford to lose.

"Della?"

"Yes?"

"You get to me, too." He spared her a glance. "We're going to have to talk about that someday."

"But not today." She lifted her phone. "Today—tonight, I need to get sharp on Crawford before we get to the office."

"That's fine." He looked entirely too happy. He knew she didn't want more. She knew he didn't want more. They had to keep things the way they were or they could end up with nothing. How in the world could she stand her world without him in it?

"Della?"

She didn't dare look at him. "Mmm?"

"Quit worrying and just read."

He knew. He always knew. She loved and hated that. "Reading."

Two pages in, she was half-sick. Three, and she thought she was going to have to ask Paul to stop the car so she could throw up.

"You okay?" His face shone green in the light from the dash.

"You said he wasn't sick, he just likes to kill. But this man is truly one sick puppy."

"What page are you on?"

"Three."

He grimaced. "You haven't gotten to the really bad stuff yet."

Della felt the blood drain from her face. How much worse could it get?

She didn't want to know. She really didn't. But if he could be her stalker…

Clasping Paul's hand, she turned to page four.

* * *

While the street was still full of festival celebrators, the reception area of Lost, Inc., had been cleared of people. The door chime echoed through the empty downstairs. Moments later, Jimmy, the most junior investigator and chief gofer, called down from the top of the stairs to the second floor. "We're upstairs in the conference room, Della."

She looked back at Paul. "I wish I felt better about this. Are we making a mistake? If it is Dawson or Crawford, we could be making targets of these people, too."

Paul paused on the steps. "You've seen Dawson's work. I've seen Crawford's. If we could do it alone, we would. We can't."

He was right. She didn't have to like it, but she would have to be crazy not to admit it. They walked down the narrow hall and into the conference room.

Madison was seated at the head of the long wooden table near the window. Her assistant, Mrs. Renault, sat to her right, and Doc, the agency's doctor-turned-investigator, next to Mrs. Renault. Jimmy couldn't take his regular seat to Madison's left—a man Della had not met sat in it. She stilled, shooting a worried look at Paul and whispered, "Who is he?" With his shaggy golden-brown hair and full jaw colored by five o'clock shadow, he couldn't be active-duty military.

"Captain Grant Deaver, an OSI officer from the base."

The hair on Della's neck stood on end. Had Major Beech reported what had happened at her cottage? "What's he doing here?"

Paul didn't look any happier about Deaver being present than Della. "I have no idea." He sent Madison a questioning look.

"Come and sit down." Madison smoothed her long blond hair back from her face. "Grant recently left the military and, knowing his qualifications, I snapped him up. He's on staff here now with the rest of us."

An odd feeling pitted Della's stomach. Madison said the

right things, but the look in her eye was at odds with her words. Something was off. Why had she really hired Grant Deaver? Unsure, Della took her seat, and Paul sat down beside her.

Mrs. Renault, svelte and sophisticated in all things at all times, opened her notebook and poised her pen, prepared to go. She had the best electronic equipment money could buy—Madison would accept nothing less—and Mrs. Renault used it. But she also still took notes by hand for her backup copy. That determination to cover all bases made her an excellent assistant for Madison as well as a fountain of information for the rest of the staff. The woman seemed to know everything about everything and everyone.

"Della, you said you were in trouble and needed our help." Madison leaned back in her high-back chair. "Why don't you tell us what's going on?"

For the next fifteen minutes, Della briefed them on Leo Dawson and the events from her past, all the way up to receiving the package tonight. It was more information than she had ever given anyone except Paul, and given a choice, she'd have elected to have a root canal without anesthetic over baring her soul to her coworkers now. But Dawson had been in her house. Or Crawford. Or someone else. And that changed everything.

"Is that it, then?" Madison asked, her expression guarded and closed.

Della had no idea how she or any of the others felt about all that they'd heard. If nothing else, this group knew how to mask their reactions. "I think that's everything."

Madison looked down the long table between Della and Paul. "So you two knew about this—that you were being stalked for six weeks, Della—and you didn't tell me?"

"I was seeking evidence."

Mrs. Renault lifted her chin. "Which is why you've reviewed all your past cases."

"Not all of them."

"All you've worked on in the last six months," Mrs. Renault guessed. "Gauging by the misshapen stacks of files in your office."

Jimmy grunted. "That's what the wreck in there is all about."

"Back to the matter of nondisclosure." Madison's tone made it evident she wasn't happy. "Not only have you put yourself in more jeopardy than is necessary, but you made the rest of us vulnerable. That's what secrets like this one do. I can almost understand, but I don't like it, and I don't expect it to happen again. Understood?" When Della nodded, Madison continued. "Paul, you being a party to this stuns me—especially if you think Gary Crawford is the stalker."

He made no move to defend himself.

"Wait." Della held up her hand. "Paul didn't know." Kind of him to be willing to take being chewed out for her, but it was wrong. "I just told him tonight."

From his expression, Grant Deaver found that interesting. Mrs. Renault hiked her left brow, a sign she wasn't at all surprised, and Madison uttered her infamous "I see," which meant, unfortunately, she really did.

"Understood." Madison addressed Della. "We've got a grip on the problem. Let's focus on a plan. You will work with a partner until the case is resolved. That's not a recommendation, it's a requirement."

"That'll be me." Paul spoke up. "I know most about Crawford and she knows most about Dawson."

And he wanted her close, to protect her. Della withheld a groan. Caring, touching and predictable, but he would be protective and that would slow her down.

"He's been in her cottage, Madison," Mrs. Renault reminded her.

Madison rocked in her seat. "You'll stay with me."

"No." Della refused. "You're on the water. It's easier to attack and harder to defend."

Deaver rubbed his jaw. "She's right."

"The ranch is safest," Paul said.

"Totally inappropriate." Mrs. Renault frowned.

"Not if I move into the barn apartment with Warny." Everyone knew his uncle, so there was no need to explain he helped Paul at the ranch.

Madison glanced between the two, then landed on Mrs. Renault. "With the security upgrades Paul did after Utah, his ranch is the safest place in the state."

Did everyone know about Paul and Maggie's incident last year except Della? Apparently, since no one asked any questions—including Grant Deaver. He shared a very personal look with Madison that drew sparks. What was going on there? "Do you think this is necessary?"

Madison looked at Della. Her bright blue eyes were laced with regret. "Yes. You move into Paul's, he moves in with Warny and you two work together at all times."

"I want to run down the shipper on that package," Della said.

"Fine." Madison nodded, Mrs. Renault wrote and Jimmy frowned. "Jimmy, you canvass the neighborhood and see if anyone's seen anything. Mrs. Renault, run Della's ex, Jeff, and let's rule him in or out. Grant, dig up whatever you can find on Leo Dawson and, Paul, you check with Maggie and see what her sources consider the latest on Gary Crawford. Let's see if we can't locate both men or at least see what they've been up to. Doc, for the time being, I'm reassigning Della's active cases to you. Mrs. Renault, assist him, as you're able. Review the files in case someone's gone rogue and turned stalker."

Della couldn't believe it. "You're yanking my cases?" She was the agency's lead investigator. Routinely, she solved three times the cases anyone else did. "But I'm at a critical stage on Horner—the missing teen, and Panedia is—"

"Critical. They're all critical, Della. But I am reassigning them for now. It's best for the clients and for you." Madison's tone signaled she wouldn't waver. "I want you focused a hundred percent on this situation until it's resolved."

"But I've already reviewed the cases. There's nothing there."

"Indulge us, Della," Mrs. Renault said. "You're a wonderful investigator, but unfamiliar eyes can be an asset. We'll work them as hard as you do."

Mrs. Renault wasn't being sarcastic but diplomatic. It'd taken Della a while to figure that out about her. Her husband had been the base commander, which was one thing all the employees at Lost, Inc., had in common with Paul. At some point in their military careers, all of them had been stationed at the base, in some capacity. Mrs. Renault's husband died at his desk and then General Talbot had taken over. She knew how to get things done quietly and efficiently, and she didn't tolerate being thwarted.

Seeing the proverbial writing on the wall, Della nodded and admitted, if only to herself, that this was all good. Things were working out for the best. Just the thought of spending the night alone in the cottage, knowing her stalker had been there, touching her things…it gave her the creeps and scared her out of her skin.

"Good," Madison said, seemingly as fresh as she'd been when the long night had started. She glanced at her watch. "I apologize for the lateness of the hour, but we do have one more urgent matter to discuss."

Della had sensed it, and now she knew something wasn't just off, but way off.

"There's more?" Jimmy asked.

"I'm afraid so." Madison touched a hand lightly to Mrs. Renault's poised pen. "No notes on this one."

Della cast Paul a worried look and saw it reflected back in his eyes. Never before had Madison told Mrs. Renault not to take notes. Typically she'd stop intermittently during a discussion and ask if she'd gotten everything.

Madison stood up and paced a short path between her chair and the window, covered in heavy green-velvet drapes. "As you know, General Talbot and Colonel Dayton were here tonight for the open house."

The base commander and vice commander.

Doc rubbed at his neck. "Nothing odd in that."

"Nothing at all, Ian," Madison said. She rarely called him Doc. No one knew why, and no one else called him Ian. "But they weren't here tonight as guests or for the festival. They were here on official business."

"What official business?" Jimmy's hand on the table curled into a fist. He still harbored a lot of anger against the military. If he and his buddy in Afghanistan had had the proper equipment, they both would have walked away alive. Instead, his friend had died.

"To quiz me about myself and all of you." Madison glanced at Deaver, then at Jimmy, and settled her gaze on Paul. "Let me preface this by saying if you know anything at all, the time to tell me is now."

"Anything at all about what?" Mrs. Renault asked.

Madison stilled. "There's been a security breach at the Nest."

He cut the wires to the security light that had flooded Lost, Inc.'s rear parking lot. Now the cars stood in shadows silhouetted by slivers of moonlight that penetrated the darkness through the trees. Pausing, he listened, but only music from the street festival muted by the brick building filled the air. He stabbed the tires of all the other vehicles in the lot, then quickly finished up his work on the one that most mattered, gathered his tools and hid behind an ancient oak and waited.

The message to the others hadn't been planned, but when an unexpected opportunity arose, he happily seized it, and this opportunity was golden. Rather than convincing these people to butt out and mind their own business or pay the consequences one by one, he could put out the message en masse.

Della would learn swiftly the penalty of running to her friends for help. She'd suffer the consequences of dragging them into her problems, and bear the guilt. His whole body quivered with anticipation. She'd also know that they couldn't protect her. No one could. Not even her precious Paul.

And soon they'd all know no one could protect them, either.

THREE

"Figures." Jimmy pounded the table with the heel of his hand. "They blow security and try to pin it on us."

Doc swiveled in his seat to face Madison. "Did the commander blame us for the security breach?"

Paul clamped his jaw, and Della shot Madison a loaded glance. "Are we clear to discuss this?"

"Grant's clearance was on par with the rest of us." Madison's expression sobered. "According to what General Talbot told me tonight, everyone in this room has worked at the Nest in his or her own area of expertise, Mrs. Renault aside. She obtained security clearances by executive order because her husband commanded it."

Della had known they'd all been assigned to the base. She hadn't known they'd all been assigned to the Nest, and she certainly hadn't known about Mrs. Renault.

"This is not good." Mrs. Renault paled. "There's a reason the Nest is isolated."

She was right about that. The Nest was plopped dead center in the middle of a wooded and abandoned bombing range. Homeland Security had built a military installation around it to conceal it, not that even those assigned to that base were privy to the workings going on at the Nest. It was a monstrous structure erected on over a hundred acres and yet it enjoyed the same anonymity as Area 51. Was that anonymity for the same reasons? Della wondered. But while she had protected the Nest's computers from attack, the data generated, collected and stored there was encrypted and hidden even from her eyes. She had no idea what went on at the Nest. Did anyone else seated around the conference table? She didn't think so, with maybe the exception of Paul.

He might know; he'd worked broader areas in intelligence circles than the rest of them. Jimmy wouldn't know. He worked low-level maintenance, and certainly had never entered the core of the Nest. Madison was there as an analyst. Of what, Della had no idea, but it wasn't likely that she'd ever seen the core of the Nest, either. Doc had treated patients, but only the people working there. No reason for him to visit the core of the Nest. And Mrs. Renault surely didn't know what went on there. The former commander, John Renault, wouldn't tell his wife anything classified, and she was too wise and principled to even ask. That left Grant Deaver. Did OSI special investigators have full facility access? Not to the computers—that much Della knew for certain. What about to the facility itself? From his sober expression, she'd guess no. Yet his hooded eyes had her leaning toward a maybe.

"Miss McKay?" Jimmy asked Madison. "How exactly was security breached?"

"Someone leaked word of the Nest to the media. A male reporter went to General Talbot seeking confirmation."

"Tell me he didn't get it." Mrs. Renault seemed horrified at the prospect.

"Of course not, but his information was accurate." Madison looked at Paul. "Is there any reason anyone outside those in the highest positions of Homeland Security should even know the Nest exists?"

"No," Paul said. "When I left, Congress was unaware, and only three senior members in the administration were in the need-to-know loop." He looked at Grant. "Is that still the case?"

"Last I heard—plus the head of the Armed Services Committee. He was brought in for budgetary considerations."

Paul frowned. "Appropriations committee has to know. No one gets money without going through them."

Madison hedged. "Not necessarily. There are discretionary funds available in Defense, in multiple intelligence agencies, and the administration also has latitude. Whether or not they were tapped in the Nest's case, I have no idea. But it's possible, and there are other revenue streams."

Jimmy grunted. "So the commander issued a standard denial—to the reporter?"

"Of course." Mrs. Renault, not Madison, answered. "He has no other choice."

"So how did the reporter get this information?" Doc asked.

"No one knows, but General Talbot and Colonel Dayton suspect someone here leaked it." Madison's brow furrowed. "I have to ask. Did we?"

One by one, each of them denied involvement.

"You do grasp the severity of this situation, don't you, Madison?" Mrs. Renault fingered her pen atop her notebook. "This exceeds a simple security breach. The consequences are far more grave."

Paul asked the question on Della's mind. "Why?"

"The Nest is a vital defense mechanism in our national security. There's nothing that won't be done to hide its existence from the public."

"Why?" Madison frowned. "I was senior in analytics, and my access was limited. Did anyone here have total access?"

None did.

"What are they doing out there at the Nest?" Madison asked Mrs. Renault.

"Frankly, I don't think they're doing anything." She lifted an elegant shoulder. "But I think they're prepared to do everything."

"What do you mean?" Della asked.

"I've pieced together snippets of conversations overheard for years, which leaves a lot of room for errors and misconceptions. But I don't believe the Nest is active. I do believe it's prepared to be activated if the need arises."

"What kind of need?" Paul asked.

That question negated his knowing what was going on there.

Mrs. Renault shrugged. "That's the billion-dollar question."

"Grant," Paul said. "You're most current. What's your take?"

"You're not going to like it." His expression turned grim. "If security's been breached—and if a reporter has accurate information, it has been—then General Talbot needs someone specific to blame."

Jimmy frowned. "How about he blames someone actually guilty?"

"Talbot's up for a congressional appointment, and Colonel Dayton is positioned to take over Talbot's current command here," Grant said. "Both of them have a lot to lose. They will pinpoint blame on somebody."

Paul grunted. "I almost agree. They'll pinpoint blame on somebody not under their command. Otherwise, they're accountable and their careers take a hit. Talbot won't jeopardize his appointment, and Dayton certainly won't jeopardize getting the command. He's been after it since General Renault held the helm."

Mrs. Renault nodded. "That's true. John mentioned Dayton's angling multiple times."

Her distaste for Dayton came through loud and clear.

Grant nodded, laced his hands on the conference tabletop. "A breach by one of their own and they'll never get the jobs, and they know it."

"Even if they find the leak in their troops, they'll deal with it privately and throw one of us under the bus." Jimmy grumbled something unintelligible but bitter.

The gravity of their situation bore down on Della. "Any of us could be sacrificed."

Paul nodded. "Our lives could be snatched away in a second."

That caused a stir. They absorbed it and when they calmed down, Jimmy leaned forward, propping an elbow on the table. "Miss McKay, I am not going down so the commander and his vice get their dream jobs. None of us are. I understand security and clearances and all that, but somebody at this table has to know what goes on at the Nest. Why does it exist?"

"I don't know, Jimmy. None of us knows. But I fear we may regret not having asked ourselves that question sooner." Madison rubbed at her neck as if ridding it of a crick, and looked around the table. "It's after two. Let's go home, rest, think and then tackle this again in the morning."

Mrs. Renault began shutting down the office. The catering staff had all gone, and the downstairs looked normal again. Della and Paul left through the rear entrance hallway, and near its end, at the door to the street, she whispered to Paul, "Well, we know now why Madison brought Grant Deaver on board."

"*On board* is a relevant term," Paul said. "She doesn't trust him."

"No, but she is attracted to him."

"Definitely. I'm guessing she hired him to prove we're innocent."

Right now Talbot and Dayton needed an outsider. The staff at Lost, Inc., was the perfect target. Any one of them would do. Della frowned. "So, why did Talbot issue her the warning?"

"Hoping to get us to turn on each other. That someone would expose someone else for anything they can tie the breach to that clears themselves."

"Basic tactics, I take it."

Paul nodded. "Elementary, but routinely effective."

Della tapped her clutch against her hip. The night air was heavy, humid, cloying. "I hope Madison has no illusions. Whatever Grant learns, he'll feed right back to Talbot or Dayton. Probably both."

"She knows. Bringing him into her circle is risky, but it's also smart. Deaver will report to Talbot that she's trying to find the truth, and so are we." Paul turned toward his SUV.

Della shot out an arm and blocked his path. "Stop."

He did, his key fob in his hand. "What's wrong?"

"It's dark." The rear parking lot was never dark. She fished out her phone, opened the flashlight app and aimed at the pole light overhead. The glass was intact. "Must be a burned-out bulb." She lowered the beam. It flashed on a yellow concrete curb marker. "Your tires are flat." A chill crept up her backbone. "All of them."

Paul visually swept the lot. "Everyone's are. Warn the others." He started toward his SUV.

Dread dragged at Della's stomach. "What are you doing?"

Paul shot her a worried look over his shoulder. "Dawson bombed your mailbox. I'm checking out the car."

The others pushed the door open to exit the building. "Stay back!" Della herded them into a group just outside the back door.

"What's wrong?" Madison asked.

Streaks of fear shot through Della. "Someone's flattened everyone's tires."

"Oh, no," Madison yelled out. "Be careful, Paul. Mrs. Renault, call the police."

Della looked over. Mrs. Renault was already punching buttons on her phone.

"It's probably just vandals. The festival brought out the locals and the thugs, but with everything going on…" Della shrugged.

"It's dangerous to be dismissive," Mrs. Renault finished and sniffed. "Especially after the Utah incident last year. Maggie and Paul were nearly killed."

Did everyone know what happened last year except her? "How?"

Madison answered. "Gary Crawford bombed Maggie's car.

He flattened her tires, too, but she didn't notice that until after the fact. If she hadn't started her car with her remote, she'd have been in it and killed instantly."

Paul! Oh, no. Della couldn't lose him, too. He was thinking about Dawson. But with his skills, Crawford was the greater threat—and Paul knew it. The truth dawned. He was protecting her. "Paul, wait!" She ran across the lot toward him. "Wait!"

She stopped beside him. "Calm down and don't touch anything," he said. "The ground is clear of trip wires. If there's a device, it's on the vehicle."

Della dragged expertise from memory and shined light into the car. "Nothing visible." She glanced over at him. "When this is over, I'm going to chew you out. You suspected Crawford the minute I said the tires were flat."

"Not now, Della." Paul dropped down onto his stomach on the asphalt and reached back for her phone. "I need light."

She passed it to him. He swept the undercarriage with the beam and suddenly stopped. "There it is."

Her mouth went dust dry. "C-4?"

"Silver salutes rigged to ignite the gas tank."

Simple and common—anyone could get fireworks—but deadly. "What did he use for an ignition device?"

Paul flicked his wrist, scanning the vehicle's belly with the beam of light. "Wired to the ignition—and as backup, a pipe bomb."

Pipe bomb. Like Dawson. "But no remote trigger?"

"No."

Della shouted back to Mrs. Renault, "We need a bomb squad."

"Stand down," Madison yelled back. "Right now—both of you."

They were safe. With nothing to ignite it, the bomb was dormant. Della backed up anyway, and Paul stood, then swiped at the grit clinging to his tux.

A straggler group of festivalgoers made their way down the

side street. "Jimmy," Della called out. "Get them out of here. Keep that street clear."

"You got it, Miss Jackson." He took off running.

"I'll get the alleyway." Grant headed in the opposite direction.

Della wiped at the road grime clinging to Paul's shoulder. His tux was as wrecked as her nerves. "Don't do that to me again."

Paul pressed a fingertip to her lips. "Don't tell me not to do what I can to keep you safe. What kind of man would I be?"

"One who tells me things so I can help. One who knows two heads are better than one, and just maybe together they can keep us alive."

"You're angry."

"Yes." Of course she was angry. Her emotions were in riot. Who wouldn't be angry? "Don't be so cavalier with your life."

"Careful, or I might just think you care about me."

Her fingers curled into his lapel, bunching the fabric. "I do care about you."

"I mean…never mind." He brushed his face to her cheek. "I care, too."

"Fine way of showing it." She hugged him hard, rested a cheek to his shoulder for a long second, then forced herself to back away when all she wanted to do was hold him closer to keep reassuring herself that he was safe.

"Maybe you should stay mad at me. Other than dancing, it's about the only way I can get you into my arms."

"Not funny. You scared me."

"Sorry." He gave her a gentle squeeze. "But your hugs are pretty nice, Miss Jackson." She reared back and he gave her that lazy smile.

Who could stay mad with that smile aimed at them? Vexed, she rolled her eyes. "It's a good thing I'm not dating you or I'd really be ticked right now." Who was she kidding? She cared, he cared, they cared. The bond between them went far beyond dating. But the moment she admitted it, he'd run. He always ran. Not that she wanted to admit it. She didn't dare risk more than friendship. There was also his faith to consider, and it was central in his life. It was no longer a part of hers, and that could create nothing but obstacles. But all of that aside, she would never fall into the love trap again—she didn't dare. So why did knowing there were a fistful of obstacles that would doom a more-than-friends relationship between them squeeze her heart and make her want to weep?

Paul swiped at his chin. "God is full of tender mercies."

The fire department arrived first. Two police cars pulled in just after the small truck, and a van that housed the base's bomb squad stopped abruptly right beside it. Three men poured out. None of them were Beech or those who'd been at the cottage with him.

Paul succinctly briefed the team leader on the device and rigging, ending with "We need photos."

"Sure thing, Paul."

He walked over and joined Della and Doc. "Do you know him?" Della asked.

Paul nodded. "From Vet Net."

So this squad was civilian forces. "Ah." Della pivoted.

Time crept. Stilled. Then crept again. Finally the bomb squad finished and left. Soon thereafter, Jack Sampson, the mechanic Mrs. Renault had called, returned with repaired tires. He'd grabbed coffee at Annie's Café and recruited help. Now Jimmy and Paul worked with him to get the tires back on all the cars.

They finished at the break of dawn, and the police finally cleared them to leave.

Jimmy joined them. "Cars are ready to roll. I think I'll hang here. Hardly worth the drive home before we're due back."

"It's Sunday, Jimmy," Paul said. "Go home, sleep and we'll meet here at three."

He looked at Paul. "Want me to hole up here with Della while you hit the early service at church?"

Della hadn't been to church since Danny's death, and Paul never missed a Sunday. Everybody knew it. "I'm fine on my own," she said. "Both of you go."

Mrs. Renault moved toward her car. "My apologies to Pastor. I'm going home."

Della watched her go. Mrs. Renault was tired, of course—dawn had come and gone—but she still carried herself as if she'd just stepped out of a magazine or off a runway. She was one of those women who would be lithe and elegant at ninety.

"The bomb squad took my SUV for tests. We're stranded." Paul turned to Jimmy. "Can you give us a lift to Della's?"

"Sure thing."

They piled into Jimmy's truck.

When they arrived just after seven, Della and Paul got out of his truck and Paul leaned close to the window. "Thanks, Jimmy." He tapped the truck frame. "Wait to return to the office. You need rest. Best get it at the church."

"Yes, sir."

Della headed up the sidewalk. "I want to grab some clothes and things." Gracie waved from Miss Addie's front porch. Della waved back.

Paul did, too, and smiled. "Expect a call from Miss Addie."

"Definitely." Gracie would report that they were just getting home from the festival, still dressed in their formals, though they weren't fit for anything beyond the trash bin now, and Miss Addie would be calling to see what had happened. "Word will be all over the bay by the time church is out."

"With the Sampson clan doing the repairs, it's out already—about the tires and the bomb."

"True." Della unlocked the cottage's front door and started to enter but couldn't lift her foot. It was as if it rooted in the porch floor. She tried again, and it still wouldn't move.

"You okay?"

He's been in my home. Her stomach knotted.

"Della?"

Snap out of it! "I'm fine." *He's not here now. Move. Just move.* She couldn't do it.

Paul stepped to her side. A gray smudge discolored his jacket, and his tie dangled from his pocket. "When a woman says *fine,* she's anything but."

Too perceptive. Della looked over at him. "Sometimes I wish you were a little less attuned to how women think." Standing close, she frowned at him, their breaths mingling. "What do you want from me, Paul? Tell me."

His expression went flat. "You want me to answer that right now?"

"Yes, I do." She needed to know.

He studied her face, the depths of her eyes, and the expression in his burned sincere. "Today, I just want you to be safe."

Evasive. Uncommon for the straight-talking Paul Mason. "What about tomorrow? Five years from now?" She braced a shoulder against the door frame. "Will we still be friends five years from now?"

"We'll always be friends." The tension in his expression eased. "You can't trudge through all we've been through together and just walk away like nothing happened."

That was the opening she sought. The one that had worried her from the moment she realized the truth about them. It'd eaten at her on the ride home, and it wasn't going to let go. Knowing the stalker had been inside her cottage had her hesitant to enter. But Paul had entered her heart, and that terrified her far more. "I'll be in your way. If you're tied up with me all the time, how are you ever going to find a wife and have a family?" He wanted that more than anything and had said so many times.

A shadow slid over his face. "Do you not want to be friends anymore?"

"No! Of course, I do."

Relief washed over his face, and the skin around his eyes crinkled. "Good, because I'm not giving you up." He swept his jaw. "Yet we do have a dilemma." He glanced up at the porch ceiling for a second, then back at her. "I guess if being tied up with you hinders my wife-and-family prospects, then you'll have to do it."

"Do what?" He couldn't be saying what she thought he was saying. That'd be crazy.

"You'll have to marry me and mother my children." He sounded calm and reasonable, but there was a twinkle in his eye.

Her knees nearly collapsed. *Marry him?* He was joking. He *had* to be joking. But that twinkle in his eyes made her uncertain. What did he really mean? "Did you hit your head on the asphalt or something?" Serious or kidding, this was an insane solution for two people who were decidedly not dating. Not to mention his running from women who were interested in him, which he did do consistently.

"No, I didn't hit my head." He shrugged. "You worried you'd be in my way and now you don't have to worry anymore. A solution's waiting anytime I want to snag it."

Not worry? He had to be joking…didn't he? Of course he did…but…

"Don't look at me like I've lost my mind, Della. You're not in the way of anything on any front and so long as we keep you safe, I'm content." Doubt clouded his eyes. "How about you? Are you content?"

She had been content—until he mentioned the *M* word. Reeling. That's what she was. Reeling and confused and not sure of anything except the idea that he wanted her in his life. But one day… *Marriage?* Her? The idea hung over her head like a threat.

Paul smiled. "You look like you've seen a rattlesnake. I think I'd be offended—some actually consider me a pretty good catch—except, I know why you've got that look. Ease up, okay? We've got enough issues to resolve without adding my future to them." The smile faded. "We're good. I mean, I'm good. Aren't you good?"

Too good to be true—because *they* were too good to be true. He *was* a great catch, and the woman lucky enough to spend the rest of her life with him *would* be getting a treasure. But the two of them together? Something flared in her chest. It left her curious, enticed and full of fear. He needed—and deserved—a woman who would love him with all her heart. After losing Jeff and Danny, her own was shattered. "I'm good. But just so we're clear, I couldn't step in and marry you—or anyone else—Paul." He said he was just reassuring her, but he sounded serious, so she needed to be clear. She owed him clarity and honesty and so much more.

"I understand, Della. Problem solved and we can forget it. Who knows? Maybe the right woman will come along. But if not, maybe one day you'll want to marry me."

Her throat went tight. "You deserve far better than me."

He brushed a stray lock of hair back from her face, the look in his eyes tender. "Let's just forget about this. If we become a problem, I'll let you know."

She opened her mouth to object, but what did she say to that? Could she forget about it? Not replay the prospect in her mind, not allow little visions of that future to dance around in her head. Even as she rebelled, they drew her. It was going to take work. Maybe a lot of work. Maybe even more work than she ever could have imagined. "Good idea," she compromised, staying honest. "It was a pretty unexpected solution."

"Was it really?" Another smile that shook her to the tips of her toes.

What did that mean? Kidding again? Serious? Either way, the idea should have her breaking out in hives, and she might later. But right now all she could think about was having him at her side every day for the rest of her life. Oh, it'd be so easy to want that. So easy…and so wrong. If he walked out on her, she'd lose her heart and her best friend. He was all she had; there was no one else. Not anymore. "I meant it was a good idea to just forget it for now."

"Absolutely." He straightened away from the door frame, signaling the conversation was over.

Let go of it and focus, Della. She uncrossed her arms but still hesitated at the door. "You said all that to sidetrack me. So I'd forget for a minute someone wants me dead and he's been in my house."

"I didn't. You initiated the subject, not me." Paul softened his gaze. "But I'd rather see shock on your face about us than fear of him. I can't stand to see you afraid."

She was afraid, and she wanted to be annoyed but she couldn't. She took in a deep breath. The monster had been in her home and touched her things. He'd violated her and her sanctuary. "A home is supposed to be a safe harbor. He had no right."

"No, he didn't." Paul curled his arms around her, pulled her close. "You will feel safe again. I promise. We'll get beyond this."

"Will we get beyond it?" She looked up at him, her arms circling his waist. "Every time I think I can begin again and make myself some kind of life, something else happens. When will it stop, Paul? When will I ever get beyond it? Will you ever get beyond Crawford? And what about your sister? Will Maggie be running until that monster is caught or dead?"

"One day at a time."

"It's too much. Sometimes a day is just too much."

He stroked her face. "Then an hour. A minute. Whatever it takes."

Paul was right. This wallowing in despair wasn't a solution. "It is what it is."

He nodded, brushed his lips to her forehead.

Too tender. "I'm starting to wonder if anyone ever really gets past anything."

He didn't get it. The events that had shaped her life weren't going to change. How could she change? Broken was broken, and some broken things just can't be fixed. "You know, it's probably impossible."

"I'll tell you a secret." He whispered close to her ear, "With God all things are possible."

Once she, too, had believed that. Then Danny was murdered and that ended that. She pulled away and walked inside. Just inside the door, she looked around.

"Everything look okay?"

"So far."

Paul watched Della closely, hoping he hadn't overplayed his hand. Looking at the living room, he had serious doubts. *Still empty.* Beige walls. White sheers at the window and not a stick of furniture in the entire room except the lone rocking chair. He frowned. "You've been here three years. When are you going to furnish the place?"

"Whenever." She walked through the hallway and up the stairs, heading to her bedroom.

Long minutes passed. Upstairs, she was silent. He walked to the bottom of the stairs and shouted up, "You all right, Della?"

"Fine."

"Another fine." Grumbling, he went to the kitchen. It was as bare and empty as the rest of the cottage. No appliances on the counters. No canisters or plants. Nothing personal marring the glossy granite surfaces except a misshapen stack of envelopes that littered the far edge of the center island—her mail. All unopened. He glanced up to the pots hanging on the overhead rack. Their bottoms gleamed, still bright and shiny and unused. No surprise there; Della didn't cook. But even the microwave looked untouched. He popped open the fridge door.

A dozen Chinese food cartons, two bottles of water and lots of empty space.

"Della, what are you doing?" he asked in a whisper. "When

are you going to forgive yourself for being alive and actually live?"

His heart squeezed, pinched tight. *Help me help her.*

Fast footfalls sounded from the stairs. He closed the fridge as she hit the bottom landing. She'd changed into jeans and a white blouse and carried a black weekender case. "I need new locks." She stood board-stiff and a wild look flooded her eyes. "He's been back."

Surprise shot up Paul's neck, tingled in the roof of his mouth. "He's been back?"

"Things are missing. Personal…clothing things." Her face burned red.

"Show me."

Paul followed her up the stairs and into her bedroom. Bed, nightstand and lamp and dresser. No toss pillows, no bedspread, just crisp white sheets with hospital corners and not a crease. No personal items sat atop the dresser. No bottles of perfume or cosmetics or other stuff women used. Bare glossy tops, freshly polished.

She opened the top dresser drawer. It was empty. The one next to it. Also empty.

She didn't look him directly in the eye. "He cleaned out all my undergarments, even my socks."

Paul processed that. Smelled something fresh. Fabric softener? "What about the closet?"

She did look at him then. "Untouched as far as I can tell."

"Okay, let's go." He reached for her, and she brushed past him.

He didn't take it personally. She felt violated in a way only a woman violated could fully understand. She needed to be in control. Paul let her.

Downstairs, he called Jack Sampson's brother, Ken. He was the best locksmith in North Bay and a part-time volunteer at Florida Vet Net. They spoke briefly, and then Paul stashed his phone and told Della, "He'll be here after lunch."

She nodded. "Thanks."

"Are you sure the items weren't missing before the note?"

"They were here when I got dressed for the festival. The package had to have been mailed before then to be delivered late yesterday." She frowned. "But Gracie saw the guy with the box leave at midnight. He could have waited for us to leave last night, come in and written the note—he remarked on the cartons in the fridge—stuffed it in the box and then resealed it." She shrugged. "That's the only way I can see everything happening in one trip."

Paul nixed that. "The seal wasn't broken and there's no evidence of retaping." His stomach muscles knotted. "He's been here twice."

She rubbed her arms. "Can we go now?"

"As soon as we call the police and get this on record."

He checked the front door lock, and they went outside. Gracie still sat on Miss Addie's porch. She was drawing on a sketchpad and watching a man in a broad-brimmed straw hat wearing an October Fest T-shirt push a mower over the lawn across the street. "I need to check your car. You stay on the porch."

"Don't even do that to me." She set down her case and started up the driveway toward the garage. Looking back over her shoulder at him, she said, "I've had the same training—" Something snagged her shin. She tumbled and went down hard, face-first.

"Trip wire!" Paul flung himself over her, covering her head with his arms.

The garage exploded.

FOUR

"Are you hurt?"

Della frowned at Paul. What an amateurish mistake! "Only my dignity, but my garage and car are history."

Flames still flared high in the sky and licked at the walls of the garage. The entire front side of it had blown out, littering the drive and lawn with debris. The car had exploded and stood engulfed in flames. A gaping hole in the roof funneled out thick ash and billowing black smoke, and heat stretched through the distance and filled the air with a charred stench. Her nostrils burned, her skin heated.

Paul got up, offering her a hand.

She clasped it, scrambling to her feet on legs so shaky she feared they wouldn't hold her. Neighbors flooded the street. How had they gotten out there so fast? Had she been knocked out? She didn't think so, but...

"Della! Della!" Miss Addie came running across the yard, half dragging Gracie. Her silver hair bobbed and the edge of her apron flapped in the breeze. "Thank heaven. The fire department is on the way." She looked Della over and then Paul. "Are you really all right? You look all right—"

"We're fine, Miss Addie." Della smiled to reassure Gracie.

Paul swiped at a brush burn on the right side of his face, where he'd kissed the concrete protecting Della's head. "We're fine."

"What's going on?" Miss Addie was nothing if not blunt. "I know you just got home less than an hour ago."

"I told her," Gracie confessed.

"Of course you did," Della said, then looked at Miss Addie. "We were at the office in a meeting."

"I heard mention of a vandal there last night."

"He slashed everyone's tires." The mother in her refused to bring up the bomb in front of Gracie.

"Tires and more, though he didn't mess with anyone parked next door at my café." Miss Addie nodded, letting Della know she was aware of the bomb on Paul's SUV. "Is this more of the same?"

"Appears so." Paul and several other guys kept everyone across the street, away from her cottage. Both, Della suspected, in case of a secondary explosion and to negate the destruction of any residual evidence—not that she expected much of it as hot as the fire burned.

"One of your cases?" Miss Addie asked.

"I'm not sure yet," Della responded, but the last thing she wanted was to encourage questions she wasn't prepared to answer. Why the trip wire? Obviously the intent wasn't to kill her but to scare her. Create a spectacle. Show her he could do what he liked.

"Dawson?" Miss Addie persisted.

"Maybe." At this point, who knew? Though he and Gary Crawford seemed equally suspect. Was Dawson this skilled? With Internet access, he could be on a device like the one used on Paul's SUV. They needed to know more about the device here to determine what skill level was required. "I'm so sorry about your garage."

The thin woman gave Della a strong hug. "You're okay. That's what matters."

Gracie craned her neck.

"What are you looking for?" Miss Addie asked.

"The man mowing the grass. He left the lawn mower running. Why'd he leave the mower running?"

Della darted a glance across the street, saw the running mower and called out, "Paul!"

He came over, and she relayed what Gracie had said.

Paul squatted to get down to Gracie's eye level. "I saw him, too. You were drawing him, weren't you?"

"No, I was drawing pumpkins." She tucked her chin to her chest.

"Why were you watching him?" Paul asked.

"I don't know." She shrugged a slender shoulder. "He made me feel funny. Kind of creepy."

"Did he say or do anything to you, Gracie?" Her elbow burned. Della rubbed it and discovered another scrape.

"Where was he, hon?" Miss Addie wrapped an arm around Gracie's shoulder. "Which house?"

She pointed to the cottage directly across the street. "See his lawn mower?"

Miss Addie's eyes narrowed. She darted her gaze from the mower to Della and then to Paul. "That cottage is empty."

"Lawn service?" Paul asked.

"Not likely. I own it, and I ain't hired nobody to cut the lawn."

Della sent Paul a loaded look "Gracie, what did the man look like?"

"He had on a big hat."

"What color was his shirt?" Paul asked.

"Orange. It matched the little flowers." She pointed to marigolds.

"It was an October Fest T-shirt," Della said. "I saw it from the back, but not his face. Was he wearing jeans?"

"I dunno. But he had on blue shoes."

"Blue shoes?" Paul grimaced. "Are you sure?"

She nodded, looking up at Paul. "I never seen shoes that color before."

He glanced at Della. "I'd better report it."

Della nodded. Gracie might have seen Della's stalker again. Had he returned to silence the child? Her landlady had lost a husband, then her only daughter to breast cancer, and Gracie's father to the war. She didn't need to risk losing more. "Miss Addie, it's a good time for you and Gracie to go visit your sister."

Quick on the uptake, she nodded. "It is."

"We'll wait while you pack."

"Gracie—" Miss Addie patted her shoulder "—we're gonna have ourselves a real-life adventure."

"We are?" Her face lit up.

"Yep. And it starts right now. We leave in ten minutes, so wait by the driveway and plan what you'll want to stuff in your suitcase while I chat with Della a second." When Gracie got out of earshot, Miss Addie asked, "Where you gonna be until this jerk is caught?"

"Not here." Telling her would only put her and Gracie in more jeopardy. "You can reach me through Madison."

"Same here." She snorted. "If it was just me, I'd stay, but not with Gracie."

"No, not with Gracie." After Danny, Della wouldn't advise or allow any parent to take chances.

Miss Addie hugged Della hard. For a thin woman many considered frail, her grip was surprisingly strong. "I'm worried about you, dear heart."

Della was worried, too. A stalker *and* the Nest security breach. One would have been more than enough, but two major challenges at once? "Have Jimmy check your house. Make sure when you ran over here, Blue Shoes didn't run in there."

Nodding, she called out, "Jimmy!"

He came running to her. "Yes, ma'am, Miss Addie."

"Take a peek in my cottage, and make sure that varmint supposedly mowing my lawn over there didn't slip in on me. I'd hate to have to shoot him, it being Sunday and all."

He took off, high-fiving Gracie as he sprinted past her, then disappeared into the cottage.

"You watch your back and Paul's, too. That viper Gary Crawford likes to blow up things as much as Leo Dawson." She frowned. "It ain't him, is it?"

"I don't know who it is. But I'll watch our backs," Della promised.

The fire department arrived, along with the police, and the neighbors lingered on the street. Some had pulled out lawn chairs as if at a ball game. They sat in clusters and chatted. Someone brought out iced tea, someone else, snacks for the kids. It was turning into a block party.

People here seemed to take whatever happened in stride. Why the cops didn't insist they go indoors until they searched and cleared the neighborhood, she had no idea, but they didn't.

Twenty minutes later Miss Addie and Gracie left the subdivision. Jimmy was right behind them, making sure no one followed them out of town.

Two hours later, Della and Paul finished up with the police and reports and the cottage had been deemed safe. Della informed her insurance company and Madison and Mrs. Renault, who had already talked with Miss Addie about getting repairs lined up. When the last of the authorities had gone, Paul turned to Della and said, "It's time to take five."

"Too much adrenaline to even think about it right now. It's still gushing through my veins." She swiped her windblown hair from her face. "I called and updated Mrs. Renault. She's arranging all the repairs for Miss Addie since she's gone. Now I want to check out the package shipper, but I need a rental car first."

"Emma's sending one." Paul looked up the street. "Should be here any time."

Emma. Florida Vet Net's Mrs. Renault. "Can you take me to get a car? Then you can get to your office or do whatever you need to do." She felt horrible, keeping him tied up as she had and away from church and his work.

"I'm not leaving you. We're checking out the package. Then we're meeting Ken Sampson—"

"Who?"

"Ken Sampson, the locksmith," Paul said. "Then we're going to the ranch. Sound like a plan?"

Relief shamed her. She was a grown woman and alone. She shouldn't rely on him. But relying on him felt good. Not facing all this alone felt better than good. It felt great. And that made it all the more important she stop it. It wasn't fair to either of them. She could never be what he most wanted—a wife and mother and woman of faith—and she couldn't dare want anything ever again. She couldn't survive another loss. Her precious Danny was dead and no matter what anyone said, it was her fault, just as Jeff had said. She was his mother. In all things, her first responsibility was to protect him, and she failed. Pain swelled in her chest and her heart hollowed. "Thank you, but—"

"No buts. We're in this together. Crawford or Dawson or anyone else—it's us, Della, not just you, and on the other problem—" he referenced the security breach "—I've got as much to lose as you."

It was them. This wasn't just about her, and he was right about the Nest breach, too. Who knew which of them would be tagged for sacrifice? While what he said should have scared her to death, it actually made her feel better. The need for them to work together wasn't wholly a matter of her reliance on him. He was also relying on her. The joint effort was a necessity for them both and, in the matter of the security breach, the team effort was essential to him and to everyone at Lost, Inc. She could live with that. "Rental's here."

"Good." Paul headed to the CRV being parked at the curb, taking off his cummerbund and removing his jacket. He'd lost his tie hours ago, and now he rolled up his once-white shirt-sleeves. "I feel like a fool running around in a penguin suit at ten in the morning—especially one as grimy as this. Want me to grab your mail or did you get it yesterday?"

"No." Della shot a glare at the mailbox. "Please, just leave it. It's probably fine, but honestly, for now I've had all the excitement I can stand."

Hiding in plain sight.

It was one of many skills he'd learned and put to good use in the past couple of days. Thrilling in an odd way, but watching Della hit that trip wire had been exhilarating. For a minute, it looked as if she'd spot it and foil his plan. But she'd gotten cocky, giving Mason the what-for about wanting to protect her. Silly mistake. But predictable. So she'd tripped the wire and set off the explosion. He relived the pinnacle moment again in his mind—and watched them pull away from the curb in their rental.

You were afraid, Della. But I know you. This, me being in your house, knowing I could have killed you but chose not to. He chuckled. *That's nothing compared to what you're about to discover. You think you're so strong, but you're weak. Soon you'll know what fear really means.*

She'd be dysfunctional. Totally unable to do anything for fear it'd be the wrong thing. *Scared still.*

His body tingled. *I can't wait.*

Della tapped her sunglasses at the bridge of her nose. "Mrs. Renault said the shipper was in Panama City." She reeled off the address and set the GPS.

"Just over an hour." Paul tapped the turn signal and moved into the right lane, pulling in behind a white truck. "Hungry yet?"

"I'd better wait until my stomach stops shaking."

"Okay." He clasped her hand. "We got sloppy, Della. We're lucky to be alive."

Sloppy? "Too full of myself is more like it." She spared him a glance. "I won't make that mistake again."

"I know it irks you when I get protective." He rubbed the back of her hand with his thumb. "I wish I could say I won't do it anymore, but we both know I will, so I won't. It's just that…"

"What?"

He shrugged, draped an arm over the steering wheel. "Later. This is definitely not the time to talk about it."

Talk about what? Now he had her curiosity up. "If there's one thing I've learned in the last three years, it's to seize the moment. It might be your last."

"Ouch. Fatalistic."

"Truth is not always kind or gentle. It is always truth."

He conceded the point. "Okay, but I'm not sure you're ready to hear it."

Getting away from the cottage had her feeling more like her old self rather than a hunted victim. "I'll get ready."

He kept his gaze fixed on the road. "I've been thinking about our conversation on the porch."

She wasn't ready. "You've decided I'm right and want to put some distance between us—as soon as all this is over?" She braced for an answer she didn't want to hear. What if he said yes? She'd mourn him forever.

"No." He glanced over. "You matter, Della. You've always mattered." He put both hands firmly on the wheel and squeezed. "From the first time I heard your voice, I knew you were special, and you are."

Her heart lurched. "Paul, you know I can't—"

"Hang on. I'm not pushing you into a relationship you don't want. I'm just saying you matter to me." His Adam's apple bobbed. "It hit me at the cottage that with the explosion, the debris could have been deadly."

"I guess it's good I was distracted and klutzy."

"Yeah, I guess so." The smile faded. "I won't ever lie to you, either. Or leave or blame or abandon you. Not today, not ever." He cleared his throat. "That's all I wanted you to know. As long as I'm alive, you're not alone."

The intensity in his voice rocked her world. All her ex-husband had done that hurt her so deeply, Paul had promised not to do. What did this mean? Did Paul love her? No, he'd definitely not said that. Or maybe he had. Maybe he loved her, but he wasn't in love with her. Big difference. Confused, she tried to wrap her mind around this. In three years, he'd never said anything remotely close. She had no idea what to do with this confession or what it meant. "Is this related to your faith?"

He laughed. "Sort of. When I was in crisis, I tried to shun faith, too. Like you, I felt God had failed me. But it worked out that faith was the very thing that pulled me through it. He gave me the strength I needed." Paul passed a blue truck, a white Honda, then turned and whipped into the drive-through at Starbucks. "But it's related to me as a man, too." He grunted. "I understand you and where you are inside. The lack of sleep is getting to me. Want some coffee?"

Her mind reeled. She couldn't slot all her thoughts, so she just nodded.

"Your usual?"

"I have a usual?" One he knew?

He hiked an eyebrow and placed the order. "Two grande Caffè Mistos. Two-percent milk. One with two sugars, one with one Splenda."

When he passed her the cup, she took it. "I guess I do have a usual."

"You order it every time, Della."

"You don't." She hadn't realized she knew that. What else didn't she realize she knew about him?

"You noticed." He smiled, genuinely pleased. "You haven't said anything about what I told you." He sipped from his cup, set it in the holder, then put the car in Drive and returned to the road. "Did I scare you?"

"After the night and morning I've had?" He'd scared her

silly. Not in the way the stalker did. But scary stuff all the same. She was an abandoned woman consumed by guilt and shame, one who'd determined that living her life alone was the only way she could function from that point on. And then a man she respected and admired and whose company she enjoyed because it was no threat to her, and, well, because he was special, unloaded by saying she mattered and he might ask her to marry him one day when he knew she never wanted to marry again. It knocked a woman off her feet. Not swept. Body slammed. She had no idea what to do with all that. Or even an opinion on what she should think about it beyond one thing, and that one thing scared her more than everything else.

She wasn't alone.

Knowing loss, knowing grief, how in the world could she cope with not being alone?

Two blocks off the beach, third in a strip mall of a dozen stores, Della spotted the sign for The Shipping Store. The stalker had chosen well. It was a high-traffic area peopled with tourists: perfect conditions for self-absorption, noninvolvement and fast turnover. Odds weren't looking good for getting solid information here.

Della walked in with her cell phone in her hand, and approached a long gray counter. A woman standing at it wrote a check and then passed it and her driver's license over to the young uniformed clerk. A toy poodle bobbed its head out of the purse swinging from her arm.

The male clerk, a redhead with freckles and a flat nose who couldn't yet be twenty, scribbled down something and then passed back her driver's license and receipt. "Thank you."

The woman smiled at Della on her way out, and Paul, who'd dropped Della at the door and then begun the search for an elusive parking slot, came in.

Della pulled up the email on her phone and waited for the clerk to put the woman's package behind the counter.

He looked at her and smiled. "Hey, you're back."

A chill ran through Della. "Excuse me?"

"You're back. We don't get many return customers. Tourist town, you know. Well, except maybe year to year."

"You've seen me before?"

His smile faded, and uncertainty replaced it. "I'm sorry. Weren't you in here a few days ago?" He sounded confused.

Paul seemed troubled by the recognition. So was she. She looked at the clerk's name tag. "What did I do here a few days ago, Sammy?"

He stammered, sputtered and then clammed up. "My mistake. What can I do for you?"

"You can answer my question." She smiled and removed her sunglasses. "There isn't any trouble, and I'm not a cop."

"You mailed a package." He lifted his hands. "That was it. But if it wasn't you…"

She passed her phone. "Can you tell me if this is the package I mailed?"

He looked at the photo Beech's team member emailed her. "Looks like. That's my code on it, so I took it in for shipping."

Paul stepped forward. "The shipping originated here, then?"

"Yes, sir."

"You handled it personally?"

"Yes, sir, I did." The young man swallowed, bobbing the knot in his throat. "Like I said, my code's on it."

"And the person who brought in the package for shipping was this woman?" Paul lifted a hand, signaling Della.

"I'm not saying it was her. But it sure looked like her when she had her sunglasses on. She had on a big floppy beach hat, too, but her hair was the same color."

Della stayed quiet, but a sinking sense of dread dragged at her.

Paul continued pressing the clerk. "Same height, weight, general build?"

Sammy nodded. "She's not a cop, but are you? Because if

you are, I already told the cops everything I could remember one time already this morning."

Chills swept up her back. Della looked at Paul. He frowned. "Call NBPD."

Della stepped away, made the call and soon returned. "It wasn't them." She turned to the clerk. "Sammy, was it Panama City Beach police?"

"No, ma'am. I know them. This guy was plainclothes. He didn't actually say from where. But he had a badge and everything."

Della jotted down his description, and then Paul asked, "Is there anything else you can tell us about the woman? Did she pay with a credit card?"

"No, sir. From the code, it was cash." He looked at Della. "You bump your head or something?"

"Or something." Her mouth was stone dry.

"It wasn't you, was it?" Sammy's lips flattened.

She didn't answer.

"If it wasn't, then you got a twin running around here."

"What name did she put on the return label?"

He pulled the paperwork and looked. "None. But she signed the receipt."

"Can I see it?"

"Sorry. I can't let you do that."

Della stepped forward. "If you think I shipped it, you can let me see it."

"Was it you?"

"I'd like a copy of the form that goes with this shipment, please." She pointed to the photo on her phone.

"Okay." He ran a copy and passed it to her. "Since it was you."

She put the copy in her purse, then looked him right in the eye. "It wasn't me, Sammy."

"I'll make a note on that," Sammy said, swallowing hard. "And I need that copy back."

"No." They'd both covered their bases in case of testimony. "Can you describe for me again the policeman who came in this morning?" Often, the second time revealed more specifics.

"Well, there were actually two of them."

"Tall, short?" She tilted her head. "How'd you know they were cops if they weren't in uniform?"

"I told you. They had badges. I didn't catch the print on them. They were just average-looking guys in suits. Short hair, sunglasses, nothing special about them to recall."

Nondescript. Infamous for FBI, but OSI was possible, too. Beech might have followed up. Or Talbot and Dayton. Likely she would never know. "Thanks, Sammy." Della walked out of the store, stopped under the black-and-white-striped awning and clutched at her stomach.

Paul met her outside. "He really believes you shipped that package, Della, and after giving you the copy—"

"I know. To cover his backside for breaching someone else's privacy, he'll say it was me, which is why I made a specific point of saying it wasn't."

Paul touched her upper arm. "Are you all right?"

Her stomach quivered like a swarm of angry bees buzzed in it. "No, I'm not all right." She dropped her hands to her sides and looked up at him. "I'm being stalked *and* set up, Paul."

"Yes." He grabbed her arm and guided her toward the car. "But for what?"

"It depends on who came in here posing as police."

Paul opened the car door. "Maybe Beech. He does have the evidence in his possession. He could be covering his back."

"I thought of that." Della slid into her seat, buckled up and dropped her handbag onto the floorboard.

Paul walked around and got in. The door hinges creaked. He looked haggard as if he'd aged ten years since walking into The Shipping Store. "What?"

"I do think you're being set up, and I'm wondering if it isn't for the security breach at the Nest."

"So the stalker and the car bomb and the package—that's all…what—from their perspective? I sent myself the package? Why would I do that?"

"To shift the focus from you to a phantom stalker you created so you could get out of the limelight on the Nest breach."

Della gasped. "Paul Mason, I know you don't believe that."

"Of course not." He clasped her hand. "But what I believe isn't significant. What matters is what we can prove." He frowned and cranked the engine. "Someone went to a lot of trouble to make sure that clerk identified you as the package shipper, Della."

"I didn't do it. The package was shipped on the eleventh. I was in the office all day on the eleventh."

"All day?"

"All day. I was reviewing files, updating them, trying to see if I could peg my stalker."

"The stalker would know that."

"You would think." He seemed to know everything else.

"So maybe he's trying to prove that you're not you."

"He's stalking me and giving me an alibi after he fakes a shipper that looks like me? Why on earth would he do that?"

"That's a good question. Unfortunately, I can't answer it. But he made sure we'd track the package to this store through the oddity on the return address and shipping label. And he made sure the woman looked enough like you to be taken for you. How's the copy signed?"

She pulled it from her purse and passed it to him.

"Della Jackson." He grimaced. "Whatever the reason, this proves we better find out."

It did.

"But first, we need fuel." He checked his watch. "Let's grab some lunch on the ride back. Then we'll meet Ken at the cottage."

The locksmith. "You drive. I'll update Mrs. Renault." Della

dialed, got Mrs. Renault on the line and briefed her on the odd events at The Shipping Store.

"I don't like the sound of this, Della."

True to form, in Mrs. Renault's understated way. "I know. Why would someone make out like they're me when I've got an airtight alibi for that time miles away?"

"I'm not sure. But everyone at Lost, Inc., being under suspicion of the security breach won't help. It undermines the veracity of your alibi. I'm going to brief Madison and Grant on this, but my instincts say this is a deliberate assault on you, to undermine your character and put a strike on your Class-C license."

"You think he's doing this to create enough doubt to get my license yanked?"

"Perhaps." Mrs. Renault paused, then added, "I'll check with Madison, but it's probably best for you to lie low for a time and let us sort some things out."

Della's eyes felt gritty and the early afternoon sun glaring off the cars on the road in front of them wasn't helping. Paul braked for a red light. Mrs. Renault's suggestion made sense, but… "We're grabbing lunch and then meeting the locksmith at the cottage," Della told her. "Then we're going to get some rest."

"Good idea. Stay put until you hear back from me."

"I'm not going to find answers…there." She didn't say the ranch. If the stalker had hired someone to impersonate her, and if there was a connection between these incidents and the security breach at the Nest, the odds were high her phone was tapped. Lost, Inc.'s, too.

"Park and stay on the sidelines, Della. We'll move as quickly as possible."

"Thanks, Mrs. Renault. Is Doc having any problems on my cases?"

"We're progressing there, as well."

"Okay." Della ended the call, feeling deflated. For three

years, she'd given her job her all, everything, holding back nothing and giving nothing to anything else. Yet in less than a day, her cases were progressing well without her. *So much for making a difference. Being indispensible. Doing anything important.* That rattled her to the core.

Just what kind of purpose was there in her life? Was there any? Did anything mean anything? Or was she just treading water, taking up space?

"Hey, you okay?" Paul sent her a worried look.

"I'm fine."

"Fine. Again." He sighed. "When are you going to say what's really going on in your head?"

"Trust me, you don't want to know." She put on her sunglasses and looked out the window, feeling small and insignificant. Helpless and more than a little hopeless.

"I want to know or I wouldn't have asked."

She exaggerated a sigh. "I'm wondering why I'm here. I'm wondering if my life is worth anything at all. And I'm wondering if after I get some sleep I'll still be wondering."

"Ah." He turned off the highway and onto the road leading into North Bay. "That's pretty heavy thinking considering the night and morning we've had."

"Yeah. It is."

"Well, set it aside for now and let's get lunch. Boat House okay? You love their pecan-crusted grouper."

She did. "Do you notice everything?"

"About you?" He smiled and the look in his eyes warmed. "Now and then something slips by me."

Too intimate. And she liked it too much. Wary, she quipped, "Then I don't have to wonder about my life. I can just ask you."

"I work with vets in crisis every day. To do them any good, I have to be aware and observant. I wouldn't be much good if I couldn't answer a lot of those kinds of questions." He sent her a loaded look. "You ready for my answers?"

She wasn't. She really wasn't. That teasing comment about

marrying her had changed everything. She didn't see him the same, and she couldn't hide from the fact that he saw her differently, too. A new awareness simmered just beneath the surface between them. She didn't want it. But she did like it—and she hated liking it. Absolutely, she was not ready for his answers. "Can we just eat instead?"

"Of course." He pulled into the Boat House parking lot, then into an empty slot. "Della, you've got to stop worrying about what I said and about us—no, don't deny it. I see it in you." He cut the engine. "Everything will work out."

Would it? Could it? A glimmer of hope that it would work out had her fighting not to run as fast and far away from him as she could. "You're bent on protecting me from everyone, including myself, aren't you?"

"I'm bent on seeing you happy. All of this will sort out. You enjoyed the festival party. I find that encouraging."

"I'm having an identity crisis in the middle of a stalking crisis and a setup and you're encouraged?"

"Yes, Della." He clasped her hand and squeezed. "For the first time in three years, you're admitting you have an identity and you're finally—I've prayed hard for this—getting personal. We're actually talking about us. That's progress."

Us. That had her shivering. "Quit analyzing me."

"Just observing, not analyzing."

"Well, stop it, okay? Your timing is really bad, Paul."

"You're ticked." He smiled. "I like a woman with fire in her eye—though I have to say, I'd rather it wasn't searing the skin off me."

"Then back off and it'll stop."

"All right. But ask yourself if there's ever a good time. You're the one who said don't wait, say what you have to say because it might be your only chance." He cut the engine and got out of the car. "You don't have to answer me. I promise that I won't bring up us or your life again—until you do."

"Fabulous." She rolled her eyes because it was expected but

seriously felt relief—and worry. What exactly was Paul doing? Why? She'd not intruded into his personal life, but if he could intrude and put comments out there about marriage, then she could ask questions. "Your parents were friends first. Did your father just announce to your mother that if their friendship got in his way of finding the right wife, she could just marry him herself? Is that why you did that?"

"Actually, my mother told my father they were getting married and when and where to show up."

"You're kidding."

"No. She decided, he agreed, they got married and that was that."

"Well, it's worked out fine for them."

"That was my thinking."

So that's why he'd tossed out that volley. To gauge Della's reaction. "When you were growing up, were they happy?"

"With each other?" He grunted. "Definitely." His expression sobered. "They've always been crazy about each other."

What wasn't he saying? "But…"

"But they were so crazy about each other that they never had room for Maggie or me. I pretty much stayed out of their way. I thought it was me. You know what I mean. Then Maggie came along and they didn't make room for her, either."

The mother in Della rebelled. "They didn't embrace their own children?"

"They liked to pull us off the shelf when it was convenient and then put us back on it and ignore us when it wasn't." He reached for the car door. "It mostly wasn't convenient."

Della's world had revolved around Danny. She couldn't relate to this. "That must have hurt you and Maggie both."

He gave her a resigned look. "It was normal. When something has always been that way, it's normal. You don't miss what you don't know and have never had."

The pain behind those words floated to her on the warm air. It had hurt. It still hurt. "But you made sure Maggie never felt that way. You made her the center of your world." Maggie and Madison McKay had been best friends their whole lives. Madison often talked about Paul's devotion to his sister—and how she wished her brother and she could have been as close.

"I made sure Maggie always knew she was loved. I always will."

Simply stated. Elegant and heartfelt. Della stretched across the center console and hugged him. "You're a good man, Paul."

He grinned playfully. "It's about time you start appreciating me."

Della sat back. "I've always appreciated you. I've been lost with you. I can't imagine going through all we have without you."

"You're not lost. You never have been. We're just taking the scenic tour." He touched a fingertip to her jaw, dragging it to her chin. "You're a good partner for the journey."

"You, too." She smiled. "It'd be a better one if we knew what this stalker is trying to do to me and why."

"We'll get there." He lifted the door handle. "But first, let's eat."

FIVE

Inside the restaurant, the hostess seated them against the back wall. It was the best table in the house, facing the bay. Several boats bobbed at the pier, boaters who'd ridden in for lunch. In North Bay, it was common to take boats rather than cars on jaunts to waterside businesses.

The waitress took Della's order. "Pecan-crusted grouper, hush puppies and salad with blue-cheese dressing."

"And to drink?"

"Sweet tea."

Paul ordered the amberjack and Della watched the interaction between him and the waitress. She was drawn to him, and he was polite and respectful, but no more. Yesterday, Della would have assumed the reason he wasn't interested—the woman was pretty and she seemed nice—had to do with women all wanting something from him. That was a hazard when you had it all: looks, charm, money and sense. But today, she knew better. Now she felt bad for him. Paul wanted a family. After what he'd revealed about his parents, she realized his family had been him and Maggie. His parents had just shared the house.

Della had had family. Jeff. Danny. And it'd been wonderful. They'd been so in love and devoted to each other...until it was gone.

Which of them—Paul or her—had it worse, she couldn't

say. But it seemed it'd be easier to not know what you were missing. Having and losing…you knew exactly.

Some holes in life are just dug too deep to ever crawl out of.

Paul spread his napkin in his lap. "You okay?"

She should say fine, but knowing he took exception to her doing that, she couldn't. Smoothing her own napkin on her lap, she sighed. "I want to talk about my life."

He smiled. "That was quick."

"It's your fault. Dragging up all this stuff."

"I haven't said a word."

He hadn't. That surprised her. She sighed. "With everything that's happened, I'm tired and half-crazy. Ignore me."

"You're pulling away again." Disappointment flashed over his angular face. "Why, Della? Don't you trust me?"

"I do." She didn't like it, but truth was truth. "It's not that." Dragging her fingertips over the hemmed edge of her napkin, she curled its edges. "It sounds like a pity party even to me."

"Can I decide for myself?"

If he hadn't asked, she might have refused him. But this was Paul. He hadn't insisted or pushed, and he'd understand and give her an honest reaction. She took a sip of her iced tea. "I've lost everything and asked for nothing. Yet I still can't catch a break with both hands and a net."

He nodded but said nothing, forcing her to let it drop or to go on. She went on. "Why is this happening to me, Paul? I do my job, I do the best I can do with my clients and I give it to them straight—good or bad. I don't cause trouble, don't deliberately hurt anyone else or cause other people problems…well, not on purpose, anyway," she amended, remembering Gracie's tears. "So why does this bad stuff keep happening?" She parked her chin on her hand. "I just don't get it. I can't even get a picture of my baby. Not even one photo. He ignores the judge and takes off long enough for the police to figure he's gone for good. If I tried that, they'd slap me in cuffs so fast…" She choked up.

Paul reached over and clasped her forearm where it met

the table. "You can't control Jeff's actions. Only yours. You're doing your best to be your best. That's all you can do. But—" he leaned forward and dropped his voice "—I do have a question for you."

No answers. A question. "What?"

He looked her straight in the eye. "How do you know these things happening aren't meant to protect you? Nothing's hurt you yet. Scared you—certainly scared others around you and me, too—but you tripped over the wire coming up the drive instead of going out the back door as you typically did. You avoided injury in the car. You noticed my SUV had flat tires. I didn't. We both could have been seriously hurt, but we weren't. And you saw that zip code discrepancy on the package. How many times do we get packages and not even glance at the labels?"

"What's your point? That God is watching over me even though I don't believe in Him anymore?"

"I believe He is," Paul said. "But that wasn't my point." He leaned closer. "Look at what could have happened versus what did happen. In each case, you were aware and that awareness prevented something much worse from happening."

"So you're saying I should have a little faith. In myself and in God."

He smiled.

The waitress arrived with their food. Della's stomach growled, and she pressed a hand to it. She'd always been a person of faith. Always believed she was being watched over and protected—until the incident. When Danny died, she'd felt abandoned and betrayed. Why hadn't He protected her son? Why? Was it something she'd done? Not done? She just didn't understand.

By the time the waitress left, Della had regained a little balance. "God left me, not me Him, Paul. Him and Jeff."

He stilled, stared at her a long moment. "Jeff left you, yes." Paul cut into the slab of amberjack on his plate. "The way he did it—meeting you at the airport with the divorce papers—that's pretty hard to forgive."

"I can't, but you could?" Is that what he was saying?

"I honestly don't know." He chewed a bite, then swallowed. "I hope I could see that he was grieving and lashing out. Pain can make you do that in ways you never thought you would. And Jeff had to be looking for someone else—*anyone* else—to blame." Compassion filled Paul's eyes. "He was holding his son. He opened the mailbox." Paul paused and visibly shook. "Can you imagine the guilt he felt about that? That he, who was responsible for protecting his son—the son you trusted him to protect—failed and he lived but his baby didn't?" Paul stiffened. "Jeff was seriously injured but he lived. Danny died. The man wouldn't be human if he didn't try to put blame somewhere else. Maybe it's not right or fair, but it is human. Imagine this whole incident—witnessing it firsthand—through his eyes. He had to be…"

"Devastated." Her eyes blurred. In all her replaying of this in her mind, never before had she stepped into Jeff's position and seen the events through his eyes. Why hadn't she done that?

Pain. Hurt. Loss. Grief. So many reasons to explain his blaming her, but she was supposed to love this man as much as he was supposed to love her. They should have turned to each other, not against. He'd failed Danny that day. But Jeff had also failed her. And in a way, she'd failed him, too. That's what she saw now that she hadn't seen before today. It changed things. The back of her nose tingled, her eyes burned and a knot lodged in her throat. She hadn't cried since she'd buried Danny, but she was painfully close to doing so now. "You're a compassionate man."

"Compassion and faith come together. It's hard to have one without the other."

She pushed at her salad with the tines of her fork. "I had that once. That connection that let me see things like this. But it's

gone now." Now anger and outrage and confusion and emptiness filled that space. So much emptiness.

"I don't believe faith comes and goes."

"You don't?"

Paul shook his head. "It's a choice you make." He signaled
the waitress for more tea.

Or a choice you don't dare make. No way could she try to
fill the empty places. It hurt too much to fill them and watch
them empty and disappear. People, possessions, emotions—
no matter how much you tried to protect them and yourself,
you couldn't do it. You couldn't, and then you had to suffer
the loss and failure. She'd suffered enough. She had nothing
more to give or to lose.

Her chest went tight and she sought solace where she'd
hoped to find it so often before. Pretending to be occupied
with her food, she recited the poem in her mind....

*Mother, do not weep. Do not despair. Do not regret. The
child now absent from your loving arms rests in arms more
loving. Strong arms where no tears are shed, no sadness or
struggles are borne, no illness suffered and no pain endured.
Wise arms that heal and protect, foster contentment and abundant joy. Be at peace, Mother. Your child is happy, safe and
content. Your child is embraced in unconditional love.*

What she would give to believe it. To be spared the heartbreak for one second—just one second—when she believed it.

But she didn't. *Fake it till you make it.* Three years, and she
was still faking it. How long would it take? How long before
she stopped dreaming of giving everything she had or ever
would have just to hold her baby in her arms one more time?

Overcome, she pulled her napkin from her lap, then snagged
her purse. "Excuse me a second."

She rushed outside, into the warm noon sun, yet her bones
felt cold-soaked, her heart ravaged. *Why?* If God was real and
He loved her, then why?

Having no answers, expecting none, she stiffened and

turned on the sidewalk away from anyone coming or going, and faced the wooded lot next door.

Something slammed into her.

Propelled forward, she lost her footing, fell facedown on the sidewalk. She looked up and saw a boy about thirteen hop off and then grab his skateboard. He'd plowed into her. Boy, if God did exist, He had some sense of humor.

"I'm sorry," the boy said. "I didn't see you." He reached down and helped her up, then handed her back her handbag.

"It's okay." She brushed loose bits of shell and concrete from her hands and sleeves. "Just be more careful next time."

"Yes, ma'am." He skated off.

"Della!" Paul came running down the wooden Boat House steps. "Stop him." He zoomed right past Della. "Stop. Hey, you on the skateboard, stop!"

The boy looked back, his yellow shirt flying from its tie at his waist, then pumped hard, putting as much distance between himself and Paul Mason as possible.

Della caught up to Paul. "What are you doing? You're scaring that kid to death."

"Give me your purse."

"What?"

"Your purse." Paul snagged it, forced it open.

Della jerked it back. "What's wrong with you?"

"The boy put something in your purse."

She looked inside. Her hands shook. She shook all over and a groan escaped from deep in her throat.

Worried, Paul reached into the bag and pulled out a small plastic mailbox. On its side written in red nail polish were two words.

Baby killer.

Della keened.

Paul clasped her arms, hugged her to him. "You're okay. Do you hear me? You're okay." He started moving, inching her toward the rental car. "Della, you have to get yourself together. We've got to find that boy."

Seeing that mailbox… Inside, she had shattered into a million pieces. Now she struggled to gather the pieces and patch herself together. *The stalker. The stalker had put the boy up to that.*

He'd seen the stalker.

"Yes." She found her voice. "We—we have to find the boy."

They rode up and down the streets near the Boat House, and then widened the search to cover Grandview Avenue that paralleled the water. Paul pulled to a stop at the curb for the third time to talk to a resident spotted in his front yard. He got out of the rental.

"Excuse me, sir."

An old man wearing bib overalls and a red baseball cap paused raking and looked at Paul. "Yes, sir?"

"Did you see a teenage boy skateboarding past here in the last fifteen or twenty minutes?"

"Yellow shirt? Red hair?"

Della's stomach tightened.

"Yes, sir. That sounds like him," Paul said.

"That'd be Tommy Jasper. Two doors down on the left. See that red truck?"

"Thank you."

Paul rushed back to the car, got in and told Della, "He lives two doors down. Red truck."

"I heard."

"You okay now?"

She nodded. "Fine."

Paul pulled to a stop. "Please, tell me *anything* but that."

"I'm not falling apart at the seams anymore."

He smiled and touched a hand to her cheek. "Good."

Comforted by that touch, she got out of the car and they

walked to the door of the brown-brick home and rang the doorbell.

Tommy answered. "Oh, man." His eyes stretched wide and he tried to shut the door.

"Don't," Della said. "You can talk to us or to the police, but you're going to talk, Tommy."

A brawny man with beefy arms appeared behind the boy. His hair was the same flaming shade of red. Definitely his father. Paul introduced himself, then Della.

"Pete Jasper. Tommy's dad." He extended his hand and they shook.

"Tommy knocked me off my feet on the Boat House sidewalk."

"I'm sure he didn't mean—"

"No, he didn't," Della said quickly. "But he did mean to put this in my purse."

She passed the plastic mailbox and let Mr. Jasper see what was written on it.

His eyes stretched wide, then narrowed. "Tommy, what is this? Where'd you get it, and why'd you put it in Miss Jackson's purse?"

"It was a joke."

"It's not funny," his father said. "That's a mean thing written on there."

Paul interceded. "Tommy, this is important. Do you know what a stalker is?"

"Yes, sir." He went serious.

"Miss Jackson is being stalked. This mailbox is connected to that. I want you to tell me what happened. Why did you say putting the mailbox in her purse was a joke?"

"Because the man told me it was."

"What man?" Paul asked.

"I don't know him. I was riding my board by the Boat House. He stopped me and said he wanted to play a joke on her. He told me what she was wearing and gave me twenty bucks." Tommy looked at Della. "Just put the mailbox in her purse. That was all." The boy looked scared. "He said she'd get the joke. Honest, I didn't know—"

Della softened her voice. "I believe you, Tommy. The man used you. It's not your fault, though you do need to be careful about who you work for in the future, okay?" When he nodded, she asked, "Can you tell me what he looked like?"

"He's about as tall as you." Tommy hiked his chin toward Paul. "His hair was real short—lighter than yours," he told Paul. "And he had on sunglasses. His tan's holding." Tommy shrugged. "Usually by October, tans are fading out, but not his."

"What was he wearing, son?"

Tommy glanced back at his dad, his eyes darting, as if scanning his memory. "Cargo shorts and a green camo shirt. Not skinny, but almost, and the shirt was tight on his arms." He grabbed his thin biceps. "He works out a lot."

"Camo?" Della stilled. Short hair, camo shirt. "Do you think he was military, Tommy?"

"Maybe. He stood real straight."

Not the most definitive response. The man could be anyone. Tommy had described a guy that fit the description of half the men in the county. "Did you notice anything that stood out?"

"Naw. He was just a normal guy. He didn't come across as weird or anything."

Paul nodded. "Did you see his car?"

He thought a second. "No. No car. He was on foot."

"Where did you meet the man?" Paul asked.

"He stopped me on the sidewalk a little ways down from the restaurant."

The stalker was following them, and he'd had a very brief opportunity to bring the boy into this. Della's heart beat hard and fast. "Would you know him if you saw him again?"

"Sure." His expression stilled and doubt crept in. "I think so."

Della passed him her business card. "If you see him again,

would you call me at this number, Tommy? As Mr. Mason said, it's really important."

He nodded, took the card. "I'm sorry, Miss Jackson. I wouldn't have done it if I'd known he was a stalker."

Della forced herself to smile. "I know."

His dad clasped Tommy's shoulder. "We'll keep an eye out. If we see him, we'll let you know right away."

The man had that look in his eye. The one bent on protecting a woman. "Don't try to detain him," Della said. "He's extremely dangerous."

"Extremely?" Pete Jasper asked.

Paul grimaced. "He's used explosives twice already. His intent is deadly."

Tommy paled.

His father's face burned red. "We'll keep a sharp eye."

The look exchanged between the men warned to watch out for Tommy, but neither of them said anything to the teen. That wasn't safe. His dad scribbled something on a torn piece of notebook paper and passed it to Paul. *Pete Jasper* and his phone number. "Tommy," Della said. "I don't know that the man will bother you, but he could because you saw his face. You watch yourself. And no more talking to strangers."

"Yes, ma'am."

Della and Paul got back into the rental. It was sun-warmed and unlike the blistering in summer, now it felt good. "We'll ride around and see if we get lucky."

"Waste of time," Della said. She shoved her sunglasses up on her nose and scanned the backseat. "But we can do it if you want. Frankly, I need sleep— Oh, no."

"What?" He put the car in Drive and pulled away from the curb.

"Jimmy was supposed to put my suitcase in the car—when we switched to the rental—but it's not here."

"He was hopping. We all were."

"He probably left it at the cottage."

"We'll swing by and see. If not, he might have it with him."
Paul stopped at the stop sign. "I got sidetracked and didn't tell
you, but Ken Sampson, the locksmith, called when you stepped
outside at the Boat House. He's all done changing out the locks
and the cottage is secure again. He said some men were still
boarding up the garage when he left."

"Mrs. Renault arranged it. Jack Sampson's cousin Luke is
securing the garage." The auto mechanic was related to half
the people in North Bay.

"I'm worried about this stalker following us." Paul braked
and then turned onto Highway 20. "I didn't pick up on it. I
should have, and I was watching."

"So was I, and I didn't spot him, either." That was a bad,
bad sign. She frowned. "I'm usually better than this. I'm feeling like an amateur."

"You're not an amateur. An amateur doesn't solve three
times the number of cases anyone else does at Lost, Inc., and
she doesn't get branded as Madison McKay's top private investigator."

"Okay, then. If I'm good, he's better." The truth in that
hit her like a sledge. "Paul, what if the reason we didn't spot
him is that he's got the same training we've got? He knows
the tactics."

"Thinking along those same lines. But, man, I hope we're
wrong and he's not a pro." He checked the rearview. "This is
one time we don't want to be evenly matched."

An edge could be the difference in success and failure, in
survival and death. "Yeah, well, we don't always get what we
want. Instead of an edge, we've got a new worry." Della looked
over at him. "Tommy's description is vague, but it doesn't fit
Dawson or Crawford."

"No, it doesn't."

"Could the stalker be working with someone else? We know
a woman shipped the package."

"Maybe a man posing as a woman. But the man Tommy

described at the Boat House was too tall and muscular to pull off being me."

"True, and Sammy's at an age where he'd notice. The shipper was a woman." Paul changed lanes and then added, "But when he was pushing the lawn mower, he was alone." Paul made a left and braked for a runner crossing the street. "Crawford always works alone. What about Dawson?"

"Alone. Definitely. He's antisocial." Not Dawson? Not Crawford? Then who could or would do this to her? Someone working for Talbot or Dayton? Neither of them would dare to dirty his own hands. Not with those promotions dangling in front of them. Someone on one of her cases? Not likely. They'd come up dry.

That she didn't know for certain who was behind all this most scared her. The enemy was under her nose, tracking her like prey, and he was still unknown and unseen by her. She could walk past him—might have walked past him dozens of times—and not even know it.

Paul made the turn onto her street and pulled into the driveway at the cottage. He cut the engine and stilled, his expression grim and tense.

Della alerted. "What's wrong?"

"The new locks didn't hold." Paul pointed toward the porch.

She leaned over to look past the rearview mirror and took in a sharp breath.

The front door to her cottage stood wide-open.

The front door rocked back on its hinges, wide-open, mocking her.

The police arrived and, led by Detective Cray, they went through the house. One officer shouted down from upstairs, "All clear."

Madison and Mrs. Renault stood out in the front yard with Paul. Della stepped away to recommend her neighbor Jean Manning go back home with her children until they were sure the area was safe. She was prone to chatting, and Della couldn't get away from her. Half listening to Jean drone on, Della tried to key in on what the others were doing, but caught only snippets. Jimmy was working the neighborhood to see if anyone had noticed a stranger, and Doc was tied up on his cell phone with the locksmith, Ken Sampson.

Doc stowed his phone in a clip at his waist and returned to the group. "Ken didn't see anybody other than Luke, the contractor. He finished up, put the new keys inside the back door on the kitchen counter, locked up and then left a spare under a rock by the back door."

"What about the men securing the garage?" Della asked. Plywood covered the blown-out front wall, the burned-out roof.

"Luke and his men were still here working when Ken left, so I called him. He didn't see anyone else, and his crew left together."

Paul swiped at a mosquito buzzing at his arm. "Cray hasn't determined a point of entry. Or if he has, we haven't been told."

"This is getting beyond ridiculous." Madison bunched her pale blond hair at her nape and secured it with a scrunchie, then headed up the sidewalk. "Detective Cray? Where are you?"

He stepped out onto the porch. "Madison. Good to see you." His smile was broad, his teeth pearly-white. His suit was rumpled and his shoulders were straight. Nice-looking man of about forty—too old for Madison, who was barely thirty, but she had his full attention.

"I wish I could say the same, and ordinarily I would be delighted to see you, but too much has happened in too short a time," she told him. "I'm worried about Della."

Realizing she had only half Della's attention, Jean raised her voice and Della couldn't hear the detective's response, but clearly Madison didn't like it. Her smile faded, and she clamped her jaw. Whatever he had said clearly ticked her off. "Did you hear him?" she asked Jean as the detective went back inside.

"No, I didn't." The woman frowned. "Are you listening to me?"

"I'm sorry, Jean. It's a bad time. I really need to get back. Excuse me." She started to step way, but the woman continued to drone on. Surreptitiously, she inched a couple of steps closer to the group so she could better hear.

Paul looked as angry as Madison. "Nonsense."

"What did he say?" Della muttered, and when Jean shrugged, she got firm. "I really have to go now." She walked away and joined Paul.

He was tense, head to heel.

"Paul?" Della asked, her stomach fluttering. "What did Detective Cray say?"

No answer.

Mrs. Renault answered, and her habitual cool exterior was ruffled. "He thinks you're doing this to yourself. The man's shortsighted at best. Dismiss him."

"Why would anyone do this to herself?" Della started shaking. Her mind tumbled into conspiracy theories where Cray was working with Talbot and the vice commander, setting her up. Had they actively recruited the detective or was he a victim, too? It had to be Cray or Talbot—unless she was totally off base, connecting what was happening to her to the security breach at their top-secret facility, the Nest. Tag her and neither man lost his promotion. Both of them mistook grief for instability, though honestly right after Danny's death, when Jeff blamed her and then walked out, she had been unstable. But she had not been and wasn't crazy. To breach security on a classified project, she'd have to be both. Yet at this point, who could predict how far they would go? At the moment, even she didn't know what to believe, but for the fact that she was not guilty.

The problem was that sometimes innocence wasn't enough to save a person. Big fish use big bait and big hooks. To them, she was a guppy. Expendable.

Inside, she quivered, and swallowed hard.

"Miss Jackson," Cray yelled out to her. "You can come inside now."

Della started up the walk on shaky legs, hoping her knees didn't give out. Paul, Mrs. Renault, Jeff and Doc followed her.

She paused beside the detective just inside the front entryway. "If you think I'd do this to myself you're sadly—and dangerously—mistaken."

He had the grace to blush. "Just doing my job, considering all possibilities." His eyes narrowed, and any hint of shame in them vanished. "There's no sign of forced entry, but a lot of things are missing."

Paul stepped closer, put a proprietorial and supportive hand on her shoulder. "She was with me the entire time. She couldn't have done it."

"The entire time?" Cray asked.

"Yes. We went to Panama City and then to the Boat House," he said, then relayed their activities from the night before when he picked her up at Miss Addie's through the run-in with Tommy Jasper and the mailbox, closing with their conversation with Tommy and his father.

Cray's suspicion faded. "The cottage is pretty much a disaster, Miss Jackson. It's been cleared and my team just finished downstairs. They're headed upstairs now. Stay on the first level until we give you the okay to go up."

She nodded and walked inside.

"I'm afraid your living and dining room furniture's been stolen."

"There wasn't any." She looked up at Cray. "They weren't furnished."

He seemed baffled. "I thought you'd been living here three years."

"I have." She walked on.

Mrs. Renault interceded. "May I speak with you, Detective?"

"Mrs. Renault." He spared her a tentative smile. "You're looking well."

"Thank you." She clasped his arm. "Outside, if you please."

Madison whispered. "Uh-oh. I know that tone. She's going to blister his ears."

"No doubt about it." Jimmy nodded, his lips pursed. "I hate it when she gets that tone in her voice. You're doomed. I'll take a ten-mile hike in full gear over that ear-blistering anyday. But in his case, it's fine by me. Suspecting Della? He's earned it."

Appreciating the support, Della walked around the corner into the kitchen. Countertops still empty. The place did look robbed. And lonely. Truthfully, it was. Three years ago, she'd been desolate and alone. Her home reflected the way she felt. But was she the same person now as then? Honestly?

Della glanced at Paul, talking to one of the uniformed officers, to Madison and Jimmy, and glimpsed Mrs. Renault, who stood on the front lawn indeed blistering Detective Cray's ears. He was doing a lot of listening and grimacing but no talking. At least he was wise in that regard. She'd needed them, and they'd come.

And there had always been Miss Addie, who had tucked Della under her wing, not with pity but with strength and fortitude, reminding Della she could endure and grow and be strong again—it was possible. Miss Addie didn't harp on it. She'd done it herself. Twenty years ago, her husband went to the store for milk and bread and never came home. She hadn't known how to balance a checkbook. But she could cook and take care of homes, and she loved those things. Now she owned the café and a dozen cottages. She'd been a surrogate mom in many ways—keeping Della focused day-to-day, bringing her chicken soup when she had the flu—and would have been even more so if Della had permitted it.

Paul's voice snagged her ear. "It wasn't stolen. It was empty."

Paul. Who was always there, always kind and caring, always just on the other end of the phone whether it was two in the morning or two in the afternoon. Her heart warmed. She wasn't the same now as then. She wasn't alone. Not anymore. She had no family, but she had good friends who genuinely cared about her.

If God did exist, maybe He did that. Maybe He brought good people into your life to fill the empty space. If He did exist…

She'd been angry, felt abandoned. Been angry and abandoned, and she'd blamed God for not protecting Danny and her. But had He failed Danny? Or her? She had failed her son. Jeff felt he had failed them both. But if God did exist, was her life now God's way of taking lemons and making lemonade?

Having mixed feelings about that, she tucked it away to think on later and walked on. The fridge stood open. Smells of warming food filled her nose. She peered inside at the tumbled Chinese food cartons and spotted something—her stomach plummeted, coiled into knots. "Paul."

He joined her, looked inside. "Jimmy," he called out. "Get Detective Cray."

"What's up?" Madison stepped around the corner.

Della turned to look at her boss. "There's a baby bottle of milk in my fridge."

Cray returned with Mrs. Renault. "You need me?" he asked Paul.

"There's a baby bottle in the fridge."

He called over an officer. "Collect that as evidence."

"Detective," someone called out from the top of the stairs. Urgency rippled through his voice. "Up here."

He took the stairs two at a time. Paul and Della followed, their footfalls echoing like thunder. A uniformed officer stood at the head of the stairs, his face pale, his expression confused. What was wrong?

"Where?" Cray asked.

"Bedroom, sir." He motioned to Della's room.

Cray entered. "Wait here."

From the doorway, Della pegged the officer's upset.

A bloody knife protruded from her pillow.

And across the once crisp and unwrinkled white sheets scrawled in thick black marker were the initials *D.B.D.*

Cray swung around to look at Della. "Who is D.B.D.?"

"Wrong question," Paul said from behind her. "It's not who, but what does it mean?"

Cray waited.

"Dead by dawn." Della's voice trembled.

Cray's expression went dark, then darker. "Your stalker?"

She nodded.

He muttered. "Lock it down!" he shouted. "Everyone out on the porch. Now!"

Not expecting him to yell, a rattled Della jerked and stumbled into Paul.

He steadied her, and asked Cray, "What are you doing?"

"We cleared the second floor before anyone else entered the cottage." Cray's skin turned ashen. "None of this was here."

Della sucked in a sharp breath. "He was in the house with you?"

"Evidently." Cray hiked an impatient thumb toward the stairs. "Get her out of here."

Paul rushed Della down the stairs and out onto the porch. She scanned the faces of those clustered on her lawn but didn't see anyone she didn't recognize. Mrs. Renault and Madison looked worried. Jimmy was ticked, and Doc seemed baffled. From the driveway, Grant Deaver joined Madison and they walked up to the porch.

"Don't worry." Madison clasped Della's hand. "We're going to catch this creep."

Her heart still racing, her legs like water, she nodded. "First, we have to identify him."

"He's brazen," Mrs. Renault said. "Unabashedly arrogant."

"Sure of himself, to hide in here with us and the police on scene. He's trained. Rapid escalation. Intensive preplanning." Clearly looking for more characteristics to analyze, Madison worried her lower lip with her teeth. "Grant, did you pick up on anything out back?"

"No. No accelerants in the garage that should have intensified the planted explosives." He frowned. "This guy clearly knew exactly what he was doing."

Grant had been studying the garage. That explained why Della hadn't seen him or known he was here. The image of the baby bottle on her refrigerator shelf burned in her mind. "This isn't case-related, Madison. It's personal."

"Or he wants it to appear that way."

When briefed, Detective Cray agreed with Della. "Beech is going to share the test results on the knife in his possession. We'll cross-match as soon as our testing is complete." He rubbed at his neck. "What about your ex-husband, Della? If he blamed you for your son's death, then maybe…"

"I can't see Jeff doing anything like this."

"Maybe he snapped." Jimmy shrugged. "It happens."

"It does happen." The detective motioned to one of his men. "Check out Jeff Jackson. I want to know where he's been in the last six weeks and what he's been up to."

Relief washed through Della. She honestly didn't think Jeff would do any of this, but then she hadn't thought he'd blame her for Danny's death, either. She'd been wrong then, and she could be wrong now. He couldn't be trusted, and she needed to know. Still, guilt for considering him a suspect grated at her. How could she take serious offense to him doubting her and then turn around and doubt him? Yet not doubting him would be foolish, and this was different. He wasn't a couple of continents away, just a couple of states. It was possible. But surely not. Surely not probable. She looked at Paul to gauge his reaction.

Guarded, closed, maybe even suspicious, he looked away. Surely he didn't think Jeff had done this, and he had stood up for her, so he didn't think she was guilty. So what had Paul so guarded and closed?

Whatever it was, he wasn't talking. And he continued not talking for the next two hours.

It wasn't until they were in his rental and on the way to pick up one for her that she summoned enough courage to ask, "What's wrong with you?"

"Are you still in love with Jeff?" Paul spared her a glance, then focused on the road. "Is that why you haven't furnished the cottage? Are you just marking time here until he makes peace with blaming you for Danny and comes to his senses?"

Paul sounded angry. If she were doing what he suggested, why would it make him angry? "Stop the car, Paul."

He pulled over in the Publix parking lot and stopped, then looked over at her and waited.

"I loved my husband. I thought we'd grow old together," she said. If she weren't exhausted, she wouldn't be saying all this. She knew it yet couldn't seem to stop. "But love can wither and die. It can be something beautiful one day and something dark and ugly and awful the next. Betrayal can do that. I've lived it."

"But if Jeff is over that? What if he regrets what he did and how he handled it? He probably does, you know. He was injured and his son died in his care."

"If Jeff regretted anything, he'd say so." She always said he'd never get ulcers because before a little thing could be a big one, he harped on it. He'd spit out anything and everything that went through his mind, right or wrong or indifferent. "He'd send me a picture of my son." Her own had disappeared or been confiscated en route home from her deployment. "He hasn't. He doesn't regret anything—at least, not so far as I'm concerned." He probably had plenty of regrets about Danny, but those he blamed her for, so it'd be regret she happened to be Danny's mother.

"I know he hasn't, but that doesn't mean he won't. It doesn't mean he—"

"What is this really about?" She took off her sunglasses, saw her reflection in his and resented that the dark lenses shaded his eyes. She couldn't read him with his eyes hidden. "It's clear something is on your mind that goes beyond whether or not Jeff's the stalker."

"You didn't answer my question."

"Which one?"

"Is the reason you haven't furnished the cottage that you're marking time until Jeff comes back, tells you he still loves you and brings you home?"

Early on, she'd envisioned that very scenario. But as the days grew into months and then years, it had faded. Each month that passed had also changed her reaction to him showing up at her door. "I am home."

'You're not answering me."

"I thought I was pretty clear."

"Not to me." Paul stilled, his grip tight on the steering wheel. "Do you still love him?"

"Don't be ridiculous. The man I loved doesn't exist. Maybe he never did exist. I don't know. What I do know is that I was crushed and devastated and he—he promised to love me—and instead he blamed me. He severed all ties, divorced me and left me standing in an airport not knowing a soul with no one to call and nowhere to go. I had no one, Paul. My son was dead, and I stood there alone with absolutely no one. Could you still love someone who'd done that to you? Someone who was supposed to love you forever?"

"That's not the question, Della. This isn't about me. All this is worth hearing, but it doesn't tell me what I want to know. Let's keep it simple. Do you still love him?"

"No." She spat out the word. "I don't love him. I'm not waiting for him to change his mind and come get me. If he tried, which he won't, I wouldn't let him."

"Okay." Paul paused a moment as if letting that sink in. "So the cottage is bare because…?"

She squeezed her eyes shut. "Do we have to discuss this now? I'm tired, I'm scared, I'm lost and I'm so angry at being violated like this I can barely breathe. Why are you pushing me now?"

"Because I have to." He whipped off his glasses.

She looked into his eyes and saw this was not about Jeff. It was about her—and Paul. And what she saw in his eyes sent chills racing through her. She saw the one thing she never thought she'd see. Doubt.

It knocked her back in her seat. Hurt in ways she couldn't have expected it would hurt. "You think I've slipped over the edge or something and arranged all this. You—you think I'm making it happen." She couldn't believe it. "You stood up for me, but you're not totally sure I didn't hire someone to help me pull this off." Mentally reeling, she sucked in a staggered breath. "Do you think I leaked word to the press about the Nest, too?"

"Unbelievable."

"Paul?" She couldn't believe it. Couldn't wrap her mind around it. She'd trusted him. Believed in him. Dared to let him into her world when every instinct in her body warned her to never let anyone in again. "You do." Outraged, devastated all over again, she reached for the car door's handle, jerked it open.

"No, Della, wait. You've got it all wrong."

"I don't think so. I *had* it all wrong, but I'm totally clear now." She looked at the store beside Publix. A-1 Car Rentals. "I'm going to pick up my sedan and—"

"And then I'm going to follow you to the ranch."

"Uh, no. No way."

"Stop. Think. There's nowhere else to go. Madison's? Mrs. Renault's? You said yourself you'd be putting them in more danger. The ranch has the best security."

"I don't want to be around you right now. I might not ever want to be around you again."

"You're not being fair. Do I get to explain? This isn't what you think, Della."

"It's exactly what I think." She shook, gripped the shoulder strap on her purse and squeezed. "Do you think I'm blind? I see the truth in your eyes."

"Truth, maybe. But not the truth you think."

"I thought you trusted me."

Hurt rippled over his face. "You're taking this all wrong."

"Sure I am." She slammed the door and walked off.

He jumped out, yelled over to her, "I'll be waiting."

She didn't slow down or look back.

SIX

Man, had he botched that one!

Paul thumped the steering wheel with the heel of his hand and kept his eye on the front door of A-1 Car Rentals' brick building. She'd jumped to conclusions he hadn't expected—one that infuriated him. He couldn't believe she'd think any of that for a second. Three years, and she still didn't trust him. Wasn't she ever going to heal? At all? A little? Did she even realize her insult? He hadn't responded immediately. At first he'd been too stunned and then too angry. Before he recovered, she stalked off. Just stalked off, refusing to listen to his side of things. That shocked him again.

He sat, fumed and lost himself in his reeling thoughts.

When he next glanced at the clock, he was still chewing himself alive inside and was stunned to see forty minutes had passed. A-1 wouldn't be winning any customer service awards. No, something was wrong.

He rushed out of the car and hurried toward the front door.
You should have just told her.

The accusation in his mind chafed emotions already raw.
She thinks you've betrayed her, too.

When he pushed down deep, past all the clutter, hadn't he betrayed her? Hadn't he? He'd done the one thing he knew she didn't want. He'd fallen for her. She'd trusted him, and he'd blown it. She'd seen doubt in his eyes, all right. But it wasn't about her guilt or innocence. It was about his own.

He'd failed her. In a different way than Jeff had, but he'd failed her all the same.

She wasn't waiting for Jeff anymore. That was the good news.

She now doubted Paul, considered him the same kind of betrayer as Jeff. That was the bad news.

If she really understood his doubt, she'd resent him even more. That was the worst news, and there seemed nothing Paul could do about it.

The green sedan she was supposedly getting still sat parked two cars over. What were they doing to her in there? He yanked the door open and went inside.

The place was empty of customers.

A man walked out of an office and into the reception area. Thin, a white shirt, gold-wire glasses. "Where's Miss Jackson?" Paul asked.

"Oh, she left a good bit ago."

"She left?" Paul's voice elevated a full octave. "In what? The green sedan—"

"She didn't want it." He stammered, unsure why Paul was so upset. "She took the red CRV out back."

"A good bit ago?" Oh, Lord, no. She could be anywhere. Her stalker… "Can you track the car?"

"No, sir."

"You don't have tracking devices on your vehicles?"

"Not the CRV. It's new to the fleet. We haven't installed it yet."

"Give me the tag number."

"I—I can't do that." He frowned, backed up a step. "Are you a cop?"

"No." Rather than wasting time arguing or pleading, Paul called Detective Cray. He had the clout to get the vehicle information most quickly. "I need some information on a rental vehicle."

"And you're calling me because..."

"You can get it."

"Why would I get it?"

"Because Della's in the vehicle."

Cray's voice turned serious. "You were supposed to be watching her."

Guilt rammed into Paul. "I was trying to. She ditched me at A-1 Rentals."

"So she could be doing this to herself."

"No, she's not. She got upset over a personal matter. It had nothing to do with the case." Paul grimaced. "Look, she's got a healthy lead and I'm worried."

"Personal, huh?"

"Yeah."

Cray's voice changed, sobered. "Her stalker's been too active. She's vulnerable, Paul."

"I know that, and they won't give me the tag number, which is why I'm calling you. Can you help me, or what?"

"I'll take care of it. Hold on." In the background he issued the order to someone, then returned to Paul. "Still there?"

"Yeah." Paul turned his back to the counter, stared out the window. Where would she go?

"While we're waiting on that, I've got an update on her ex, Jeff Jackson. We checked with the locals in Tennessee. They did some digging and just got back to us. Best they can tell, Jeff hasn't been seen up there for over a week."

"This has been going on longer."

"Well, he could have been out of pocket longer. The woman he sees was away for a couple weeks before that, visiting family. So she's talked to him but hasn't seen him for over a month. Neither have his neighbors, but that's not unusual, they say."

"So he could be her stalker."

"It's possible, though it seems he's settled into a new life with this new woman. She says he's put the past behind him. Doesn't talk about it or anything. They're planning on getting married at Christmas. She's always wanted a Christmas wedding."

He hadn't changed his mind, and there wasn't a sign of regret. Relief and new fears merged and roiled in Paul's stomach. He could be just as angry as the day he served her divorce papers in the airport, when she returned from Afghanistan. "We have to find Della."

"In a big way," the detective agreed. A-1's phone rang. In short order, the detective relayed the red CRV's tag number to Paul, then added, "I'll put out an APB on her."

An all points bulletin would tick her off even more. "Can we keep this low-key and just locate her? The stalker seems wired in to me. You issue an APB and he knows we're out of touch with her. That could make him even bolder, and considering he's gutsy enough to strike her bedroom with a whole team of cops in the house…"

"Valid point. Low-key is safest for her." Detective Cray paused, then added, "You going to tell me what ticked her off enough to skate out on you?"

Shame washed through Paul. He watched a woman holding a toddler's hand walk down the sidewalk through the window. A lump formed in his throat. "I doubted her."

"You think she's—"

"Not about any of this. No way." A twinge hitched in his chest. "About her still being in love with her ex."

"Ah, I see."

Paul figured he really did.

His tone changed, grew more trusting. "Any idea where she'd go?"

"I've been thinking about that as we talked, and unfortunately, no." He frowned at a spot on the wall, still trying to get inside her head. "She wouldn't put anyone else in jeopardy, so that knocks out where she works and those there. That's all she does. Other than the Lost, Inc., staff, all she has is me."

"What about her neighbor?"

"Miss Addie? She and Gracie are away. Della insisted it was safest since Gracie saw the guy mowing the lawn."

"Wise move on Della's part," Cray said. "Where are they?"

"Out of state." No way was Paul telling anyone the exact location.

"You're sure Della wouldn't join them?"

"With Gracie there? No way. She'd never endanger any child."

"It's awful, what happened to her son. Seeing that bottle rattled her. I can't see her doing anything to put a kid at risk, either."

"Wouldn't happen." Paul was as certain of that as the need for his next breath.

Cray exhaled. Static crackled through the phone. "Any other ideas?"

"Not even one." The truth in that doubled Paul's fear.

She needed to rest and think.

Della drove down Highway 98, crossed the bridge to the island and then drove on to the pier. She parked the CRV in the first available slot and cut the engine. With the festival behind them, the season was over. Tourists had gone home and snowbirds hadn't yet arrived. Normally, the hustle and bustle at the beach was welcome and quieted the noise in her mind, but today she hungered for isolation. So much had happened; she needed a breather to clear the buzz from her head and sort through everything methodically. That was her only hope of making sense of events. She rubbed on some sunscreen, gathered her purse, dropped in the keys and locked the car, then hooked her shoes on her handbag and headed down to the water's edge.

The sand warmed her bare feet. The waning sun still shone

bright, glaring through her shades. Near the water, waves broke into ripples and frothy white curls teased the sugar-white shore. She sat down just beyond the water's reach and looked out on the horizon. The deserted beach was serene and calm, perfect for a rattled woman with a lot on her mind.

Who was her stalker? That was the key question. The answer would determine who was trying to set her up, duping or hiring someone to pose as her and ship the package. Whoever he was, his intentions clearly had turned deadly. One bloody knife in the package she'd supposedly shipped from Tennessee. One bloody knife stabbing her bed. Definitely deadly.

It was true that neither Dawson nor Crawford fit Tommy Jasper's description of her stalker. Yet appearances could be changed. But had they? No evidence of it.

There ain't ever evidence of something until there is.

Miss Addie's words haunted Della. Her cases had come up dry, and neither she nor Paul could see anyone on their team doing this. That left one person on her possible stalker list. Jeff. Yet something inside her refused to believe he would do any of this. He hated her. That was obvious. But hating her was easier than hating himself. He'd never harmed anyone. He was a gentle man. True, he hadn't looked or acted gentle at the airport the day she'd returned from Afghanistan, and Jimmy was right. People could snap. They could slip or experience something that pushed them over the edge and snap like a cracker.

But it'd been three years. Surely he wasn't the same now as then, either. Surely he'd gotten some of his sense back. He'd lost his son, but would harming his son's mother bring him any relief? Of course not. He was an intelligent man. He'd draw that same conclusion—once he broke free of the mighty jaws of grief. If he broke free. Some people got stuck and never broke free. Was Jeff one of them?

She thought about it. About how he processed trials and challenges. He worked through them, prayed over them. No, the man she knew wouldn't get stuck. He'd face grief head-on and get through it. He might want to hurt her, but his idea of hurting her was the kind of thing he was doing in withholding photos of Danny. Not doing what her stalker had done with Tommy Jasper or planting bombs in her garaged car and on Paul's SUV or stealing her underwear, or breaking into her cottage and slitting her bed or mailing her a package with a bloody knife. Him refusing to send her photos of their son was a long stretch from all this. Too long a stretch.

So if not Jeff, then who was left?

The Nest.

She dug her toes deep into the sand. It was odd that this whole stalker scenario was happening at the same time as a security breach at the Nest. Was that a coincidence? Or was it deliberate? She lifted her face to the weak sun and stiff breeze, and mulled that over. General Talbot's appointment. Colonel Dayton's promotion. Men had done far worse things to achieve far less. Madison's analysis fit. The stalker had planned, and he'd gone to a lot of trouble to find a woman to pass for Della, shipping that package. Was that woman involved or was she a victim, too? An innocent bystander like Tommy who had been used and had no idea what she was doing?

Gulls cawed overhead, flying in huge circles down the edge of the beach. Used to tourists feeding them, they were nudging Della into tossing them some bread. Unfortunately she didn't have any with her. "Sorry."

She lowered her gaze back to the horizon and rested her chin on her arms, draped on her bent knees. It was odd, the effect the beach had on her. When she had been stationed at the Nest, shortly after her arrival, there had been a serious hacking attempt on its computers. For fourteen hours straight she'd combatted the attack, at war with an unseen enemy in a keyboard battle that had taken all of her skills and knowledge and every ounce of stamina and strength she'd possessed. It'd been a high-stakes chess match, where she'd had to think five, six, at times even seven steps ahead, and she had risen to the challenge. The commander and his vice had watched the entire attack play out, battle by battle, and only once had either tried to interfere and direct her defense. She'd objected, shouted why the suggestion would fail three moves ahead, and they'd left their fate in her hands. She'd launched an attack that had turned the tide, requiring the hacker to defend himself, and she'd won. Victory was sweet, even if no one outside the ops center would ever know of it. Yet it had taken its toll. Wrung out and limp, she hadn't dared to go home in that condition. Jeff would have worried himself sick. So she'd come to the beach. Stared out on the horizon. The tension had left her body and she'd talked through her fears with God. She'd sat there until the sun dipped below the horizon and sank into the gulf. And she'd left feeling renewed and refreshed and gone home.

Then Danny had died. Jeff blamed her. She blamed the computer skills that had taken her away from them. And she'd dropped them flat. The only other skills she had left were those she'd acquired in the intelligence realm, so she'd used them, getting her Class-C license as a private investigator.

When she'd returned to North Bay, she had come to the beach, hoping to recapture that sense of balance and serenity, some inkling of tranquility. At best, she'd achieved mixed results. She hadn't talked to God. She hadn't felt tranquil or serene or calm or refreshed or restored. But she hadn't wanted to crawl in a hole and die anymore, and that was a step up. So she kept coming back to the beach. Again and again. Each time she'd come, she'd found comfort in leaving, not wanting to die.

Mixed results. It wasn't much. But it was all she had left, and she was grateful for it. When you're alone and empty, something is better than nothing.

She drew in a deep breath, lifted her face to the glow still visible of the sun just above the horizon. It warmed her cheeks. The breeze kicked up, blew her hair back from her face, tugged at her eyelids. She dared to close her eyes, to let her mind wander through the facts. General Talbot had told Madison about the press leak exposing the facility, the reporter having accurate information only an insider would have. Talbot clearly knew that everyone who worked at Lost, Inc., had an ax to grind with the military. Madison was a former POW. Jimmy lost his best friend, Bruno, because of orders to execute a mission without the proper equipment. While Doc had been deployed in Iraq, his wife had been murdered in a home invasion. Mrs. Renault's husband fell victim to a heart attack and died at his desk. And Della had lost her son, her husband, her career and her faith. As potential sacrificial lambs went, Lost, Inc., was a rich target. A case could be made against any of them with little effort. So why her? And what about Paul?

He was a rich target, too. Always making waves through Florida Vet Net. He had testified before Congress on behalf of veterans at least half a dozen times. Actually, that's where her pastor in Tennessee had met Paul. After Jeff had abandoned her at the airport, she had waited for hours for him to come back. When she accepted he wasn't going to, she called her pastor because there was no one else to call. He had tried to help her, but couldn't in the way she most needed help because she couldn't really talk to him. The lines were too blurry between classified information and general life information. That was normal for people in intelligence circles. Personally and professionally, too much hurt too deep. Her pastor realized the challenge before she did and contacted Paul, certain he could help her since he and Della had walked in the same world of shadows and secrets. And Paul had helped her. He'd brought her to North Bay, gotten her an interview with Madison—nothing with computers. Computer expertise, intelligence expertise had cost her Danny. Without it, she'd have been home with him. She wanted no part of them—as an investigator—and she'd focused on reuniting people with their loved ones. That helped soothe her wounded mother's heart. Gave her something to nurture. Paul had been with her every step of the way. Helped her get the cottage, talked her through long nights of grief. They'd run into each other at Miss Addie's café and eaten together, and both hated eating alone, so it became something they did that expanded to other activities. Picnics, parties, events in the village and Madison's swirl of parties she considered a required part of the job for her staff. She didn't want to get involved and neither did Paul, but you can't rely on each other and spend so much time together and not form opinions. She liked him and he her. Then she cared and so did he. It wasn't a lightning bolt that struck them. It was more like rising water. They grew close and the water filled the empty spaces. Now he might want her to marry him one day. And that changed everything. Even though he'd claimed he was teasing her, Paul Mason would never suggest marrying a woman he didn't love. He loved her—and she was afraid to love him back.

For good reason, it appeared, since he doubted her.

Her chest went tight, her throat thick. *Why did you trust him? Why did you open yourself up to being betrayed again?* And how could he seem so devoted to her and yet doubt her?

Having no answers to those questions, either, she scrunched her toes and stared mindlessly out on the whitecapped water. The sun sank lower. Her heart sank with it. The sky streaked pink and gold, muted and quiet, but her mind reeled on. She still had plenty of questions but precious few answers, and sadly, no serenity or peace.

What about Grant Deaver?

Glad to refocus, she gave him her attention. What did she really know about Deaver? Former OSI investigator. Good reputation but not necessarily a good guy in this situation. Everyone at the office figured at best he had torn loyalties and he would report everything that went on at Lost, Inc., to General Talbot. Yes, Deaver had been wounded in the alley after the tires were slashed, but that might have been a deliberate tactic to get the Lost, Inc., staff to lower its guard and accept him as one of them. After all, he'd only been lightly conked on the head. He could be a double agent of sorts, or not. Possible and probable, whether or not Deaver liked it. The stakes were high for Talbot and Dayton, and if they wanted Deaver to act as a mole for them, they'd see to it that he did it. They had the power to make things happen.

Della folded her knees and brushed at the gritty sand clinging to her thigh. What would Paul think? He knew Madison didn't trust Grant Deaver. Did Paul trust him?

Why did his opinion matter so much? She sighed heavily. Of course it mattered. She'd trusted him. Really trusted him. Really cared about him, too. Betrayal stabbed her deep. In her mind, she glimpsed images of him laughing, them dancing, sharing popcorn at the theater, sitting on the porch swing talking about everything and nothing. Paul was always so gentle with her. Rarely pushy. Never asking for more than she could give. And, being honest with herself, she couldn't deny how many nights she'd fallen asleep wondering what his kisses would be like.

Naturally, come morning she would chide herself for such absurd thoughts. But in the wee hours before dawn, when darkness threatened to swallow her and all stood still and silent, thinking of him helped her hang on until sunrise. Nights could be terribly long, yawning and stretching out before her like lifetimes that all but stood still, tormenting her with memories of all she'd lost and would never have again.

Paul had helped her through those nights. And when she'd called him during the worst of them—in the early times of horrific nightmares—to talk her through them, he always had. Just the sound of his voice had calmed her. Soothed her. Acted as a balm to her wounded soul.

Would a man who did all that betray you?

Would he? Was he just a friend?

The truth hit her. She stilled. Denied the truth. Argued. And lost.

Sometime in the past three years, her feelings for Paul Mason had grown far beyond friendship. And that truth terrified her, burned fear into places so deep inside her she couldn't even peg where they started or stopped. How had she let this happen?

He was her true best friend. She didn't want to lose him. He'd heard her out, over and again, and he'd listened. Yet she'd refused to hear or listen to him. He'd earned the right to explain. Why hadn't she let him explain? And would Paul betray her? Really? Would he? He thought Crawford was after her and put himself between them. Would a man who'd do that betray her?

Wait. Just wait. That was doubt in his eyes.

But, she asked herself now what she should have then: Doubt about what? Had she drawn the right conclusion or jumped to a wrong conclusion?

Suddenly she wasn't sure.

They had discussed Jeff many times. Many times. But this time, Paul's reaction had been different. This time, he hadn't just listened. He'd asked questions. And the questions he'd seemingly most wanted answered weren't ones about whether or not she thought Jeff could be stalking her. They were ones about whether or not she still loved Jeff and wanted him to come get her. As a friend, Paul wouldn't be most worried about her being in love with her ex. And yet he was.

She had jumped to the wrong conclusion, and she didn't want to do so again. She didn't dare make too much of this. But how could she not feel confident concluding that to Paul, this was personal? Very personal.

And that raised another question. Could he more than love her? Had his feelings gone beyond friendship and love? Was it possible that Paul had fallen in love with her?

No. Stop it, Della.

She put the brakes on that line of thought. Yet she feared it was too late. Strange thoughts that started with his teasing solution had changed everything and created a spark that now flamed inside her chest. She recognized it for what it was. And oh, but she feared it. More than she thought to ever fear anything again in her life.

It was hope.

Oh, woman. You are the worst kind of fool. He'll run from you just as he runs—

Something slammed into the back of her head.

She saw stars, then nothing more.

SEVEN

Della was missing.

And Paul was out of options. His insides had passed tense knots hours ago and now hissed like coiled snakes. Detective Cray had everyone on the North Bay force looking for her. Okaloosa and Walton counties had been alerted. Madison had everyone at Lost, Inc., hopping, and she'd recruited her sorority sisters to canvass hotels, motels and condo rentals. So far, no one had turned up anything.

Terrified, Paul pulled into Lost, Inc., parked and went inside. Mrs. Renault wasn't in her office. Madison met him instead. "Where's Mrs. Renault?"

"I sent her home hours ago—before you called in about Della. She was exhausted, Paul. She called a few minutes ago. I told her Della was missing and she's on her way in." Madison motioned to the chair opposite her desk. "You tried Della's favorite Chinese place, right?"

He nodded. "She'd eat it every meal. Well, every meal she doesn't eat at Miss Addie's." Since word had spread through the bay that Miss Addie was gone and therefore not cooking, the café was all but abandoned except for coffee drinkers taking breaks from the Della search. "Anything new from Cray?" Paul was at loose ends. Everything in him said to search, but there just wasn't anywhere else to look.

"Nothing noteworthy. They're turning over every rock, he says."

The bell chimed. Paul turned to see who was coming in. Mrs. Renault, wearing a soft gold dress and white pumps. Her hair was loose. She rarely wore her hair down and loose.

"Anything new on Della?" she asked.

"Nothing." It hurt Paul's throat to admit it, and every time he did, his heart skipped a full beat. If he hadn't been clear on his feelings for her before she went missing, he was clear now. The faith issue still stood in their way, but his heart zoomed right past it under fear her stalker had intercepted her. "We're still looking."

"You've tried Chen's, of course." She stowed her purse in her desk drawer.

He nodded. What if the stalker did have her? What if—

"Yin's?" Mrs. Renault circled the edge of her desk. "That's her second favorite."

Again he nodded.

"What about the Ritz?" she asked.

Madison frowned. "She can't be getting her hair or nails done."

"She's not," Paul said, starting to pace. "Jimmy's been there twice."

"I'm sure you went to the beach first."

Paul stopped. "The beach?"

Mrs. Renault frowned. "You should know this, Paul. You're her best friend."

"Know what?" He lifted his hands.

"Della always goes to the beach to think. Are you telling me you haven't checked the beach?"

"Where on the beach?" He dug for his keys in his pocket.

"On the island near the pier." She frowned deeper, glanced at Madison, who looked equally surprised. "Neither of you knew this?"

"Not me. Sorry." Madison shrugged.

Paul grumbled. "The woman tells me nothing."

"She didn't tell me, Paul," Mrs. Renault said. "I noticed. She leaves troubled, returns less troubled. Sand on her shoes. Smelling of sunscreen. I ask if she's been on the island at the pier, she says just to the left of it. This is not rocket science."

Madison grunted. "I didn't notice."

"Perhaps that's a sign to slow down a bit." Mrs. Renault sighed. "I'm not surprised you missed it, but, Paul, I'm definitely surprised you did."

"Why? I can't see her return to this office with sand on her shoes or smelling of sunscreen from my office at Vet Net."

"Because you typically notice everything about her." Mrs. Renault shrugged an elegant shoulder and turned her back. "Time for tea." She headed up to the kitchen.

"He doesn't notice everything. They're just—" Madison stopped midsentence, stared gape-jawed at Paul. "You're more than friends?"

"I don't know what we are." That was true enough.

"Oh, my." Madison's eyes gleamed with curiosity.

"Not now." Agitated, Paul moved toward the door. "If Cray calls, tell him where I am."

"If you find her, phone in right away."

"I will." Paul rushed out. The beach. She went to the beach to think. Why didn't he know that?

He drove as if demons were hot on his heels, crossed the bridge to the island and got to the pier. A red CRV was parked in the lot. He compared the plate to the tag the A-1 clerk had given Cray. It matched. He called Madison. "Her car's at the pier. I'm on my way out to the water now."

Paul hung up before Madison could say anything, shed his shoes and took off through the sand. He searched to the left of the pier and spotted nothing, then cut under it and looked down the sand to its right. Drag marks led down a fair stretch to a dark lump.

It wasn't moving.

He ran toward it. The closer he got, the more afraid he became. It was a person…a woman…Della!

Finally reaching her, he dropped to his knees. "Della. Della." He ran his fingers at her throat, seeking… She had a pulse. *Thank You.* Unconscious. He lifted her head and checked her scalp. Felt a huge goose egg near her nape—and saw blood. It clotted her hair, soaked the sand.

Oh, no. Please, no. Unsteady, he pulled out his phone and dialed 911.

"Della?" With fumbling hands, he tried to rouse her. His chest heavy, his heart heavier. Why wouldn't she wake up? "Della, it's Paul. Wake up, Della."

Nothing.

He should have told her.

Please, give me the chance. Just give me the chance, and I will tell her. I will.

Fear that he wouldn't get that chance set in. Desperation rode with it. "Della Jackson, don't you dare die. Do you hear me? Don't you dare die!"

Paul paced the hospital waiting room, staring at the blue padded chairs, the gray walls and carpet. When they'd arrived, Della still hadn't regained consciousness, but she was alive.

In the two hours since their arrival, her doctor, Sam Mark, had come out to the waiting room twice. So far, they'd run a battery of tests—CAT scans, blood work and an MRI—and he reported that the laceration at her nape wasn't deep. The swelling was outward, not putting undue pressure on her brain. With a "so far, so good," Dr. Mark had disappeared behind the big metal doors again.

Paul turned to Madison. "I'm going to the chapel."

She nodded. "Any news and I'll come tell you."

"Thanks." He walked down the antiseptic hallway and entered through a door embedded with stained glass. The chapel was tiny—three pews with kneeling benches and a plain wooden cross that hung on the wall above the altar. He slid into the center pew, dropped to his knees and prayed. *Please.*

He couldn't think beyond that. But he sensed he didn't have to, that it was enough.

"Paul?"

Madison stepped in. "The doctor is in the waiting room. He has news."

Her expression told him nothing. Paul scrambled from his knees and rushed back to the waiting room. As soon as he saw the doctor, he asked, "What?"

Dr. Mark smiled. "She's awake."

Madison let out a sigh of pure relief. "That's wonderful."

"Paul, she wants to see you."

"Madison—" he started, but this was one of those moments when there were no words.

"I'm calling the office. I'll let the others know."

Gratitude raced through his veins, and Paul followed Dr. Mark through the metal doors and then down another sterile hallway to a curtained cubicle. He steadied himself and then pushed back the curtain.

Della lay still on the white sheets, wearing a blue hospital gown, looking small and frail and pale. Her eyes were closed, her hands clasped over her stomach. He stepped to her bedside and whispered, "Della?"

Her eyelids fluttered open and those warm brown eyes flecked with gold he feared he'd never see looking at him again focused intently on his face. "I'm sorry."

An apology he hadn't expected, and though he wasn't sure what she meant, he assumed it was about their disagreement. "Me, too."

She licked her lips. "You look exhausted."

Paul smiled. Vintage Della. "I've been worried about you. But I'm better now." He lifted her hand into his, careful not to disturb her IV. "Are you okay?"

"I'm fin—" She smiled. "I'm okay."

She remembered his aversion to *fine* and that smile reassured him. "What happened?"

"I don't know." Her voice was thick, sluggish. "I was sitting on the beach and something cracked me in the head. I saw stars. I remember that. Then nothing until I woke up here."

She looked over at Dr. Mark. "Can I get out of here now?"

"Not until morning. You were out a long time. I'm keeping you overnight for observation."

Della frowned. Cast a wary glance at the door. "Talk him out of it, Paul. I'm fine. Really." She swung her legs off the side of the bed and sat up. "See?"

"Whoa. You're swaying." Paul lifted her legs and tucked them back under the covers. "Just keep yourself in Park for a while, okay? I need the rest."

She studied his face. "How long was I out there?"

"Hours."

"What time is it now?"

"Nearly midnight."

That surprised her. "You are exhausted, then." She settled back in. "Okay, I'll stay. You go home and sleep."

"That's not happening." Paul squeezed her hand. "I'm not leaving you."

She gave him a liquid smile so tender it made his eyes burn.

Ian Crane from the office came in. He was a medical doctor and had privileges at the hospital. "You look okay."

"I am."

"Don't take off on us again, all right? Paul nearly had a breakdown, and I fear when you're up to it, Mrs. Renault is going to blister—"

She pivoted her head on the pillow to look at Paul, winced and searched his eyes. "You nearly had a breakdown?"

He shrugged. "I was worried."

She smiled so sweetly he was tempted to kiss her. If Doc hadn't been standing there keenly watching every gesture, he might have done so.

Doc cleared his throat. "Detective Cray is putting a guard on your door. She'll be safe here, Paul."

"Yes, she will." He hardened his voice. "I'm not leaving her."

"Understood. I'll go handle the paperwork to get you moved to a room," Doc said, then left the cubicle.

Her eyes turned glossy. "You were really worried about me."

"Very." Paul clasped her hands, pressed them to his lips. "No more disappearing acts, okay? We have issues, we talk through them." He dragged his thumbs over her knuckles. "I want to look for the stalker, not you."

"I didn't intend to disappear. Just wanted to clear my head."

"Next time, give notice." He softened that edict with a gentle squeeze.

"I will." She worried her lower lip with her teeth. "I guess underneath all that worrying, you're pretty ticked at me for ditching you at A-1, huh?"

"You scared ten years off me."

"I wasn't thinking straight."

"We all have our moments. Since you lived, I forgive you." She covered their clasped hands with her free one. "I look vulnerable."

"I think at the moment, you are vulnerable."

"Not really." She lifted her chin, rubbed her head wound against the pillow and it stung. "Well, maybe a little."

He smiled, brushed a hand over her forehead, stroking her. "I discovered something while you were missing."

Skittish, she asked, "About the case?"

"About us." He bent close and looked deep into her eyes. "Do you want to know what it is?"

"Only if it's good."

It wasn't good. It was awful—for him. "You'll like it."

"Okay, then tell me."

"You just want friendship between us, and I understand all the reasons why."

"This isn't sounding good."

"I discovered that if I let things between us move beyond that, you'd see it as me breaking your trust."

Confusion and maybe a little disappointment crossed her face. "Are you telling me I can trust you?"

"Absolutely, you can trust me." This wasn't coming out right. He was falling into the same trap he'd fallen into before in the car. "You know, this isn't coming out right. But when you're on your feet again and I'm free of brain fog, we need to talk."

"Okay." She tugged at the sheets. "But for the record, I do trust you. That's why when I looked at you and saw doubt… well, I might have jumped to the wrong conclusion. You wanted to explain, and I should have let you. I was wrong." She motioned to her head. "Old tapes playing old messages that don't apply to you. If it helps, I am sorry."

"Thank you." He wanted to say more, but her eyelids were already fluttering closed. That was probably a blessing. The conversation they needed to have required not one clear head, but two. And right now they didn't have one between them.

A nurse with a stethoscope wrapped around her neck came in. "We're ready to move her up to the third floor. Give us ten minutes, Mr. Mason, and then you can come up."

"Where she goes, I go." Paul stood perfectly still.

Doc popped in. "It's okay, Paul. Go tell Madison what's going on. I'll stay with Della until you get to her room. Third floor."

"You're going to stay with her during a simple transport to the third floor?" The nurse looked stunned.

"Yes." He winked at Della. "She's my friend—and so is he." He motioned for her to get on with it…

"Thanks, Doc." Paul stroked Della's arm, then went back toward the waiting room.

Madison looked fighting mad. "Hold on, Grant." She held her phone away from her ear and asked Paul, "How's Della?"

"They're keeping her overnight, but she's okay. I'll be with her."

"Good." She gathered her purse. "I guess I'll go get busy, then."

"Busy? Has something happened on the case I should know about?"

"No, Grant—" she lifted the phone "—has been drinking the Kool-Aid, suggesting Della did all this to cover that private security issue we've discussed." Madison hiked her purse strap on her shoulder. "I need to go have a chat with him."

Ream him was more like it, judging by the fire in her eyes. "He should be suspicious. It's his job," Paul said in Grant's defense. "He's wrong, of course. But he should prove it."

"Fine." She smiled and held up the phone to make sure her voice carried and Grant heard her. "I'll let him live."

Another woman saying "fine." This, Paul did not need, and he doubted Grant Deaver did, either. "They're moving Della to a room now."

Madison nodded, clearly thinking. "I want her out of this investigation in every way, Paul. Keep her sequestered at an alternate secure location until we resolve all this. I'll contact you on your cell to keep you in the loop."

Paul stilled. Madison knew the ranch was the most secure location in North Bay. "What alternate secure location do you recommend?"

She checked to make sure they were still alone, licked at her lips and pointed to the phone, signaling she wanted Deaver to overhear them. "Remember the house in Seaside?"

Paul did. Surely Madison wasn't serious. It was on the gulf. He couldn't secure a house on the gulf. It'd take an army— which she knew as well as he did. Unsure what she was up to, he kept his comments to himself and simply said, "Yes."

"Take her there." Madison fished in her purse and removed a key off her fob, then passed it to Paul. "Here's the key." She passed it to him. "Don't tell anyone—I mean no one. And don't call in. Your phone will be tapped."

She was setting up Deaver. No two ways about it. "I'll remove the battery, Madison."

"Perfect. Jimmy brought your rental car here and we returned Della's CRV to A-1. You keep her in Seaside until we come and get you."

"Got it."

She frowned, clearly worried he hadn't gotten the real message. Paul winked, and her expression eased. The message sent had been received. He'd go to the ranch with Della as planned. Grant would no doubt report the Seaside development to General Talbot and Colonel Dayton, and Madison and the rest of the Lost, Inc., staff would set up a sting at Seaside to nail him for crossing them and expose Talbot and Dayton as the ones setting Della up—if they were setting her up and were behind all the stalker business. Regardless, the stalker attacks should cease because he wouldn't have a clue where she was or how to find her.

Clever, Madison. Very clever.

Likely this would only prove Grant Deaver wasn't trustworthy. But it was possible it'd prove far, far more....

"Why are you driving toward Panama City?" Della looked over from the passenger seat to Paul. "I thought we were going to the ranch."

"Same reason I cleared the car to make sure it wasn't bugged or rigged with explosives." Paul checked his rearview. The cop car was still behind them. Next traffic light, Jimmy should intercede. "You buckled up?"

She nodded.

"Still have a headache?"

"Oh, yeah." She dragged her fingertips over her temple. "Dr. Mark said it could last a couple days, but I sure hope not."

"Is the shot he gave you still working?"

"The pain is there, but it's dull, so I guess so." Earlier it'd had her stomach revolting. At least that had calmed down.

He passed her his phone. "Take out the battery for me."

"Why?" She took the phone and popped off the cover.

"Is your phone in your purse?" he asked.

"Yes." Her internal alarms starting firing; it showed in her eyes. "Paul, what is—"

"Take the battery out of it, too."

"Okay." She snapped the cover back into place on his phone, then fished hers from her purse and removed the battery from it. "I'm vulnerable here, and dealing with a wall-banger head-ache, and curious. I'm going to get testy."

"We need to disappear for a while." He glanced over. "You okay with that?"

Della studied him a long minute. This was a trust test, pure and simple. "Fine."

"Not fine. Tell me anything but fine."

A smile threatened. "I'm okay with that."

He rewarded her with a hand squeeze that set her heart to racing. "I take it you're cutting communications. Have you forgotten we've got a friendly following us?"

"Haven't forgotten. Jimmy's going to help us with that."

"How?" What she really wanted to know was why.

"Next red light. He'll create a diversion."

She tensed, looked ahead and saw a green truck spinning in the intersection.

Paul lowered the glass, signaled the officer following that he feared this was a trap and took off. "Hold on." He jumped the median and shot up old Highway 331, then headed fast for the Waloka County line.

The officer stopped and checked out the truck. Della watched until she couldn't see anymore. "Is Jimmy getting himself into trouble?"

"No. He'll tell the cop something went out in his steering, and it did. He'll be back at the office before lunch."

"Okay." She couldn't take the suspense anymore. "What's going on?"

"We're enacting Madison's plan."

"Which is…what?" Della grabbed the handle on the door. Trees flashed by, making her nauseated.

"Taking you to the ranch."

Nauseated and clammy. "Then why not just drive there?"

"I think because Madison and Grant got into an argument. She hasn't had time to say, exactly."

"You're not making a lot of sense, Paul."

"Oh, but I am." His eyes gleamed. "Your boss is pretty smart. She's setting up Talbot, Dayton and Grant Deaver to see if they're your stalker."

"She's making herself a target?" Della's stomach flipped. She smoothed a hand over it.

"No, she's testing Grant's loyalties." Paul hooked an arm over the steering wheel and rode out of town and then onto a two-lane paved road lined with thick woods. "If he's being straight with Madison, it'll be fine. If he's reporting to the general, she'll know it. In the meantime, you're supposed to be at Seaside, but—"

"I'll actually be at your ranch and no one will know it, including the stalker."

Della had to give Madison props. It was a clever idea. "If Talbot or Dayton don't come out of this well, they'll find a way to fry Madison. I don't like that part of this."

"They can't," Paul said. "Not without exposing themselves."

Now that the road had smoothed out, her stomach settled. The clamminess ceased. Glad for that, Della paused, thought. "I don't know, Paul. Powerful men can make things happen."

"The Lost, Inc., folks will be fine. They're professionals, too."

"They are," Della agreed, and hoped their safety proved true.

The car warmed, the ride became pleasant and smooth and the shot Dr. Mark had given her kicked in. Her eyes drifted closed, and Della slept.

* * *

"Hey." Paul's hand stroked her face. "Time to wake up."

Della opened her eyes. She was leaning against Paul's shoulder. She sat up and glanced at the clock. Forty minutes had passed. "We're at the ranch?"

"Almost." He hit his left blinker. "I didn't want to turn off the paved road and jar you to death without you being aware of what was happening."

"Ah. The road up to the house still isn't paved?" That surprised her. Paul had money. At one time his folks had owned most of Waloka County. Paul still owned a lot of it.

"It is, just not for the first five hundred feet off the highway. It discourages gawkers. They disturb the horses."

The horses! She hadn't thought of them. "Are they okay? You've been away—"

"Warny's taking care of them. As busy as we've been at Vet Net, I haven't had the time."

"I thought he was a recluse."

"He has been for most of his life. But for Maggie, he gave it up. She asked him to move in and take care of the horses. He can't refuse her anything."

Neither could Paul, and he loved the horses, too. "Giving up your time with them must be hard for you."

"Not as hard a time as the vets have when they come home and find out the life they left is gone. So many can't find jobs and their homes have been sold out from under them."

"It's awful. And I know how important the work you do is. I've lived it. I just meant it's sad you can't spend more time with your horses. You love them."

"I do." He smiled at her. "But I love the vets more."

"I'm glad." She smiled back at him. "I'm eager to see if the place has changed."

"It never changes much, but the new barn is finished."

"The roof was going on the last time I was here." Why had he stopped inviting her out? He used to do that fairly often.

Warny seemed pleasant enough, but maybe he objected to anyone coming out. He'd been a total recluse for a long, long time.

"Then you know what's changed."

Paul's ranch was two hundred lush acres out in the middle of nowhere, surrounded by deep, thick woods. A three-acre clearing sat dead center, for the house, two barns and—what was it he called those fenced-in areas where he exercised the horses? She couldn't recall. No matter. White-rail fence stretched as far as she could see, giving the horses a lot of room to roam. When she'd been out here for a picnic, she'd seen a half dozen deer. Paul said they were plentiful, as were squirrels, and back behind the house, there was a lovely natural spring and creek with clear water that was cold even in the heat of summer. It was a beautiful place. Breathtakingly beautiful.

He made a curve and braked at a gate that stretched across the road. Pressing his thumb flat on a posted pad, he waited. The gate swung open. He drove through and it closed behind them. "Yours is the only private home I know with a biometric security system," she said.

"What happened in Utah made it necessary." He frowned. "And more."

The Gary Crawford incident with his sister. "Have you talked to Maggie lately?"

"Last night, while you were sleeping. I want her to come home, but she feels she should wait a bit."

"With everything going on here, that might be a good idea. At least until Crawford is ruled out." Della rubbed at her throbbing temple. "Will she wait?"

"Yeah. She's stubborn but not stupid. I told her it was possible Crawford was stalking you."

"How'd she react?"

"About like you'd expect. Scared. Mad. Mostly mad."

Jake, Paul's rottweiler, appeared out of the woods and made a beeline for the car, barking nonstop.

Della laughed. "I think he's missed you."

"Yeah." Paul grinned. "He's rotten, but he's mine."

He adored his dog more than his horses. And for the first time, Della experienced a quiet longing that he'd adore her a little, too. She chased the thought away. What they had was special. Too special to risk losing. Especially since it was nearly all she had. Oh, Miss Addie was good to her, and the guys at work were terrific. But at the end of the day, they went home to their families. And even if invited to join them, Della never forgot that she was an outsider. They were their families, not hers. She was alone. Well, nearly. Close.

She thought she'd needed to stay alone to survive. After loving and losing, she had believed it fully. Maybe she didn't deserve more. But being nearly alone was different. Would it be wrong to want more? Just a little more? Just something?

"What's the matter?"

"Nothing." She tossed away the wistful thoughts. It was the pain medication. She'd never dare to think about such things if she wasn't half out of her head. Danny was dead. She couldn't afford to want anything at all.

A bullet whizzed past the windshield.

To the right of the car, a low-slung oak limb crashed to the ground, half covering the road.

Paul braked hard and swerved, shouting, "Jake, sit!"

The dog dropped to his haunches, ceased barking. The car stopped, half on and half off the road. Paul narrowed his gaze at an old man in coveralls standing in the center of the road, his rifle aimed right at them.

"What in the world?" Della slumped sideways in her seat.

"It's fine." Paul grumbled, opened the car door, raised his hands then stepped out. "Warny, put that blasted gun down right now—and get your glasses on."

"Paul?" Squinting, the old man walked toward him.

"Yeah, it's me." Jake sat champing at the bit to greet him. Paul tapped his thigh, and Jake lunged at him. "Hey, boy. I'm glad to see you, too."

Warny joined them. His wrinkled, leathery face disappeared under a well-worn hat. "Sorry about that. Jake was kicking up such a ruckus—"

"What are you doing, shooting without your glasses? You could have killed us."

"Ain't likely." He sniffed. "I was aiming six feet too high." He peeked into the car. "Morning to you, Miss Della."

"Morning, Warny." She smiled. She couldn't help herself. "Bit warm today, isn't it?"

"Yes, ma'am, it is that. Surprising for October."

"Don't encourage him," Paul told her. "Why'd you shoot at us?"

"You're inside the fence in a strange car, barreling up the road to the house. What am I supposed to do, hang out a Rob Me sign?"

"I told you I was driving a rental."

"No, sir." He parked the shotgun across his shoulder. "You omitted that little fact."

Paul stilled. He might have. "Well, next time, can you wait to see who's in the car before you start shooting? The trees would appreciate it."

Warny grinned. "I believe I can manage that."

"Good." Paul returned to the car. "Oh. I don't want anyone to know we're here."

Warny's old eyes gleamed. "So that's the way of it, eh? Pastor ain't much gonna like it. I don't, either. That's all I got to say on that."

"That's not the way of it. Della's in danger. I'll be bunking with you in the barn. Heaven help me."

"I see." Warny's eyes went serious. "Well, in that case, Jake, stay with Miss Della."

The dog jumped into the car, got in the backseat and parked his nose on Della's shoulder. She petted his smooth snout. "Thanks, boy."

"Sorry, Della." Paul rolled his eyes. "Jake, get out of that car."

The dog didn't move. "He's fine," Della said.

Warny pulled out a red-and-white handkerchief and swiped his face and neck. "I'm gonna saddle up Thunder—he needs the exercise, right leg's stiffening up on him—and ride the fence. Make sure no varmints have gotten in."

"Good idea." Paul got back into the car. "You want me to throw the beast out?"

Jake grumbled at Paul. Della bit back a smile. "No, I like him close." She petted Jake's scruff. He rewarded her with an arm lick. "Should Warny be riding the fence at his age on a horse named Thunder?"

Paul nodded. "Thunder's a rescued horse. His running is a slow walk. It's good for the horse and good for Warny. They'll be fine."

"So you rescue horses, too?"

"Too?"

"Vets, horses, me."

One hand on the wheel, the other on the gearshift, Paul paused. "You want the truth?"

"Always."

"I don't rescue any of you. You rescue me."

That comment echoed through Della's mind for a long time.

Miss Addie's North Bay Café was hopping. The lunchtime crowd was out in force, though the old lady and that stupid kid were nowhere to be found.

He sat in his car in the parking lot, the pod in his ear, and admitted that the device he'd planted inside Madison McKay's office might have been a mistake. The woman didn't spend much time there. He'd have been better off to plant the bug in Mrs. Renault's office.

He tapped his blue shoe on the floorboard. There hadn't been an opportunity while repairing the flats to make multiple insertions. Just as there hadn't been an opportunity to do anything but ditch the mower before that kid pointed him out to Mason or Cray.

Patience. Whatever they were up to would be clear soon enough.

He grunted. The problem wasn't patience. The problem was he'd been delayed in traffic by that stunt Paul Mason and Jimmy had pulled to ditch the cop. Now he had no idea where Della was, and that was not acceptable.

Next door at Lost, Inc., Madison whipped into the parking lot in her sleek silver Jag and Deaver pulled in behind her in his red Jeep. Apparently they were continuing the argument that had started during their phone call while she was at the hospital. Funny how nobody pays attention to a guy pushing a bucket and a mop. Della stalking herself. What a joke. Deaver was too smart to believe that, and Madison flatly rejected it. She was a smart woman. Beautiful, too. But she had moments of brilliance, and moments weren't enough. Sequester Della at a gulf-front location? He harrumphed.

Paul Mason would never agree to that. In his intelligence days, he'd risen through the ranks on guts, brains and skill. At times, he'd been beyond brilliant and he had uncanny instincts. No way would he make a rookie mistake like that if he had any other choice. And he had plenty of choices.

"You quit?" The listening device transmitted Madison's stunned voice. "Are you serious?"

"As a stroke." Deaver's voice elevated. "I don't need this job. I wanted it because I like what you're doing here. But I can't do anything worth doing if you don't trust me."

"I can't trust you," she said on a rush.

"Why not?"

"I don't want to discuss it."

"Too bad. I do."

"I can't trust you because…" She paused, her voice softening "You're getting to me, Grant."

"Well, since it's mutual, isn't that a good thing?"

"No," she insisted. "It's an awful thing—and lousy timing."

"What I'm feeling is rare, and in my book, that makes it a good thing anytime."

"Rare? Really?"

"Really."

Silence.

He was kissing her.

In the car, he smiled around the straw pressed between his lips and sipped, tapping the steering wheel.

Things couldn't be going better. In no time he'd know exactly where Della was. Exactly.

And then he'd kill her.

EIGHT

Paul's sprawling house wasn't the swanky bachelor pad Della had expected to see before her first visit here. It was a two-story, white-clapboard home, perfectly maintained and well furnished in warm tones and oversized furniture that invited guests to make themselves comfortable and to feel at home.

Della walked into the living room and couldn't help mentally comparing its welcome to her own living room's barrenness. "It's not human for a house to have this much stuff in it and still be this clean." She smiled over at him.

"It's been home for a long time. You accumulate stuff." He blinked. "Well, most people do. It's an unspoken rule, like the washing machine eating socks."

"So that's where they go. Finally the mystery is solved." She laughed because she was supposed to do so, but her cheeks went hot. In three years, she hadn't accumulated more than a couple of spare towels. Walking closer to the piano in the corner, she studied the photos atop it. There were dozens framed of Maggie and two of Paul, both taken when he was in his teens. Oh, there was a third one in back, buried in with Maggie's. His military photo, the kind taken with the flag after basic training. "Where are your other photos?"

"There aren't any." He didn't seem at all bothered by that. "Maggie wasn't old enough to handle the camera."

"What about your folks?" Their first child and they never

held a camera? She'd taken hundreds of photos of Danny—and didn't have even the one in her personal effects that had been lost in transit along with her bags when she'd returned from Afghanistan. She'd kept it in her Bible, had studied it and the Word every day. Her heart twisted. Della wrapped herself with her arms. "Didn't they take pictures of you guys?"

"Not that I recall." He started toward the back of the house. "I'm starving. Want some lunch?"

Her heart hitched. He seemed so unaffected, so matter-of-fact about his distant parents. He loved them, and he absolutely loved Maggie to distraction. But when he was a boy, had anyone loved him? Had anyone loved the man?

The reason having a family was so important to him grew clear. A little sad for him, and still woozy from the shot she'd been given before leaving the hospital, she followed him into the kitchen.

It was a long room. White cabinets and granite countertops littered with small appliances, a bowl of fresh fruit, a candy jar with what looked like a musical top—no snitching undetected from that one. Stainless double sink, double wall ovens and three wide windows behind the table. There was a gourmet center behind louver doors that stood open. "Your mother must have enjoyed cooking."

"She hated it more than you do. But my grandmother loved it."

He thought she hated cooking. Reasonable deduction, considering she ate every meal out. "So your grandmother designed this space?"

"She and my grandfather built it with lumber off the land." He was proud of his heritage, and his family. Odd, considering. "Did you know your grandparents?"

"They died when I was little. I didn't see them much. They loved to travel."

"Ah." No grandparents to love the boy, either. Della's chest squeezed. She'd give anything for the chance to love her son and his family. His had the chance and treated him as an afterthought.

Life was strange.

Together, they made sandwiches, pulled out pickles, chunks of cheddar cheese and chips. At the fridge, Paul asked, "Soda, sweet tea or apple juice?"

"Sweet tea." Della set the plates of food on the table. Suddenly tons of questions about him and his life fired through her mind. Being here, seeing him in his home in a way she never had before...why in the world did he bother with her?

"You're worrying again."

"No, not worrying. Thinking." She sat down. "I wish we'd get this stalker thing resolved—being set up irks me—but it doesn't feel quite as urgent on the ranch as it did when we were in North Bay." She smiled. "Or is that the medicine?"

"Probably a little of both." He set napkins near their plates, then took his seat, briefly bowed his head and looked over at her. "I'm glad you feel safe."

"It's wonderful out here."

His eyes widened, his jaw dropped just a touch and his eyebrows shot up a fraction in mild surprise. "You like the ranch?"

"I've always loved your ranch." She took a bite of turkey and Swiss, chewed, then swallowed. "What's not to love? It's gorgeous."

"It's isolated." He bit into his sandwich.

She snagged a chip. "More private, I'd say."

He swallowed. "Remote."

"Spacious." She bit it, relished the salty crunch.

"Not too rural?"

She laughed.

"What?"

"You think this is rural?" She shook her head. "You're so funny, Paul."

He dabbed at his lips. Set down his sandwich and took a sip of tea. "I am?"

"I grew up on a thousand acres of scrub brush. It was forty miles to the nearest store. We had to truck in water." She chuckled. "That's rural."

"Where was this?"

"In New Mexico."

He crunched down on a pickle spear. "I'm sure you hated it."

"No, I loved it." She shrugged. "It was different than this, but beautiful, too."

He seemed shocked but pleased, and stopped chewing. "So you really think the ranch is beautiful?"

"Definitely." Hadn't she ever told him this? "Especially the stream. I love the stream." He called it a creek. They'd had several group functions out there and a few picnics in the spring.

"I had no idea. I haven't invited you out here for a while because I thought you hated it and just agreed to come out of kindness."

"Why in the world would you think that?" The tart pickle puckered her mouth.

"I don't know." He shrugged. "I just thought you did."

"Well, I don't. Hmmph," she grunted. "I guess I'd better tell you what I'm thinking more often."

"That would be…good." He lifted a chip. "I'm learning you're a little hard to figure out sometimes."

But he saw inside her far too often. "Aren't we all?"

He gave her that lazy smile. "Yeah, I guess we are."

She saved a bite of sandwich for Jake. "You going to fuss at me if I give this to him?"

"No. I do it myself all the time." He grinned at the dog, sitting statue still, watching every bite they took. "That's why the little beggar is behaving. If he acts out, he doesn't get it."

"I see." She dipped her hand down and fed Jake the last bite. She reached back to her plate for a pickle spear. "Here, have a party."

"That he probably won't eat. He prefers sweet pickles."

"Me, too." Della laughed.

Paul's eyes twinkled. "I'm humbled."

"Are you?" Paul humbled was quite appealing. She tilted her head. "Why?"

"Della Jackson, letting me into her private world." He reached across the table and clasped her hand. "I hadn't given up, but I have to say I've wondered if it'd ever happen."

"I'm sorry." Shame burned inside her. "You've been so good to me and I've been so selfish with you. Why you tolerate me, I have no clue."

"I don't tolerate you. I appreciate you." He dabbed at his mouth with his napkin. "I respect you, Della. You're beautiful inside and out, and I trust you."

Her eyes burned. He was such a good man who gave so much and asked so little. "I've been selfish with you." The absence of photos of him made her feel even worse. Clearly, he'd been shut out in his own family and in many ways, she'd shut him out, too. "If you want to know something, you could just ask."

"I've picked up a lot." The look in his eyes turned serious. "There are things I'd like to know, but they can wait."

"For what?"

"You to tell me because you want me to know." His expression went cryptic. "Warny taught me that a wise man never spurs a wounded horse. Spurring a wounded woman is even dumber. It never turns out well."

She smiled, but the truth in his words wasn't lost on her. In the past, she would have resented questions, been defensive and distanced herself from him. She regretted that now for both of them. "You are so wise."

She loved his ranch. Filled his kitchen with laughter and banter and simple conversation during the typically lonely mealtime. If Paul hadn't already been crazy about the woman, those things would have enchanted him, but her saving a bite for Jake just as Paul did…that would have knocked him over the edge.

Since he was already over the edge in love and he'd finally accepted it, she had him free-falling into what he feared would be a deep, deep heartbreak pit. Falling in love with a woman bent on never loving again wasn't the smartest move a man could make. *So much for being wise, buddy.*

Unfortunately, knowing it and not doing it were two different things. Where Della Jackson was concerned, he just couldn't seem to keep his logic and brain engaged and his sense front and center. His heart had its own ideas and it was bent on swan-diving into the pit and plunging the rest of him with it to its deepest depths.

He settled Della into a guest room next door to the master suite, and viewed it through her eyes. It was a large room, with buttery-yellow walls, white sheer curtains at the long windows and a four-poster bed that had been built by his grandfather as a wedding gift to his grandmother. In those days, they were land rich and money poor. He'd cut down the oak, planed the wood and built the entire bedroom set of furniture himself. And it was as beautiful now as it had been two generations ago.

Della loved it. She ran her fingertips along the wood, oohed and aahed, and when he told her the story of how it came to be, she got really quiet. So quiet, it worried him. "Did that story upset you?"

"No." She looked down at the floor. "I guess I just wondered what it'd be like."

"What *what* would be like?"

"Being loved that much." She gave him a shy, weary smile. "I think I need to sleep for a while. I'm getting goofy in the head again."

"Hurt?"

"No, no headache. Just goofy."

Emotional, he thought. And afraid of it—or of admitting it. "You get some rest, then. I'll go check the horses and make sure Warny is okay. He's been gone over an hour. That's probably pushing it a little for Thunder."

She nodded, stepped out of her shoes and set her purse on a chair near the window. "Okay."

"If you need me, there's a panic button right beside the headboard on the wall. Just push it and I'll be right here."

"Thanks, Paul."

He smiled, left her room and eased the door closed. Jake stood waiting in the hallway. Paul pointed to Della's door. "Guard."

Jake dropped onto his haunches in the center of the doorway and sat alert.

"Good boy." Paul ruffled his scruff and then went downstairs.

In a little anteroom near the back door, he checked the surveillance cameras that filled an entire wall in the eight-by-eight room. Every inch of his land was under camera. Middle row, third camera, he spotted Warny on Thunder lumbering along the fence line. He appeared fine; so did Thunder and the fence. Scanning the other monitors, Paul didn't spot anyone or anything out of place.

Breathing a little easier, he took a shower, changed into jeans and a fresh shirt, and then headed out to the barn. Della was warming up to him. Getting used to him. Maybe accepting him.

On Tuesday, he and Della exercised the horses. He knew she could ride, and likely had ridden as a kid in their rural area, but he didn't know her skill level. Regardless, he insisted they take it easy. The last thing she needed was a fall to complicate her head injury, though honestly the woman didn't act or seem injured anymore. She wasn't her usual sharp-witted self, more pensive and quiet, but that was a normal reaction to someone being targeted and under intense scrutiny. Actually, her reaction to all that had happened was admirable. Strength under

fire and—defending Jeff, giving him the benefit of doubt—
grace under fire, as well. Della might be wounded, but this
stalker and setup hadn't broken her.

Dark thoughts about that intruded. Maybe it hadn't broken
her because Danny's death and Jeff's blaming and abandoning
her already had. Could you break the already broken?

If Paul had learned nothing else during the worst of Maggie's ordeal, he'd learned that when you've been dragged
through the bowels of despair, it takes a lot to take you there a
second time. His parents had managed to do it, skating out on
Maggie when she was clinging to life by a thread. He hadn't expected any different, but Maggie had been devastated by their
early return to Costa Rica. His fault. He shouldn't have protected her from their indifference, acting as a buffer, making
excuses. He hadn't meant to do so. He just hadn't wanted her
to be hurt and forced to accept that they were so self-absorbed
and lost in each other there wasn't room for their kids. He'd
been there and done that. No way had he wanted Maggie to
feel as worthless and unwanted as he'd felt. In the end, she
did anyway, except she'd had him, and she knew beyond any
doubt her brother loved her unconditionally. Best investment
he'd made in his life had nothing to do with money and everything to do with Maggie. She grew up sure she was loved.

But even with all that in mind, Della's situation was different. Her being under attack, in her eyes, didn't hold a candle
to her son's murder. Very difficult, if not impossible, to break
her again on anything else after she had endured that.

On Wednesday, Madison called. No activity on the Seaside
property yet. She didn't know what to make of this, but considered it too soon to draw any conclusions about Grant Deaver
or General Talbot and Colonel Dayton—though Madison did
admit she was encouraged. Grant clearly was trying to earn
her trust. Della's and Miss Addie's cottages were both fine,
and Mr. Blue Shoes hadn't come back for the lawn mower. No
new attempted attacks to report.

By the time Paul finished the call, he was certain of a few things. Madison was deeply attracted to Grant Deaver and didn't like being attracted to him. Deaver apparently was attracted to her, too, and didn't seem to like it any better than Madison. Those two developments meant this whole situation could get even more complicated. And Della's stalker clearly knew she wasn't in North Bay. With the rapidity of the attacks having stopped on a dime when she left, the stalker had to know she was out of reach. That was the good news. It meant for the moment, Della was safe, and so were those around her. The bad news was he'd be working double time to find her, and if he wasn't Talbot or Dayton or Gary Crawford, Leo Dawson or Jeff, then they didn't have a clue who he was or what to watch to see him coming.

On Thursday, Madison reported that Detective Cray had spoken to Jeff. He was at his cabin in the mountains and phoned his Christmas bride, and she'd told him the detective needed to talk with him. That he'd called Cray seemed to relieve Della, which worried Paul. She said she wasn't in love with the man anymore, but was that true? Not that Paul thought she'd lie. But she had shut out all emotion for a long time.

In her situation, if she hadn't shut down and stayed shut down, she would cry, and she hadn't cried. What would happen if she opened the door and let her feelings back in? Would she not love Jeff then? Would she love Paul?

His stomach curled. He wanted to know; he really did. But he wasn't sure he wanted to know badly enough to find out— not just yet. Every day she seemed more peaceful, happier than he'd ever seen her. And as much as he wanted to settle things between them, provided they settled well, he wanted her to enjoy that happiness more.

Della had been miserable for a long, long time.

And he was still at war himself. God stood front and center in his life. Della locked God out of her life and showed no hint of letting Him back in. What if she came to love Paul?

At some point, they'd wish to marry. Married, they'd become one. But they'd still be divided: one who believed and one who didn't. What did that do to them spiritually? *A house divided*...

On Friday, Emma, his assistant, ran into a challenge at Florida Vet Net and left a message on the office answering machine for Paul to call the office as soon as possible.

He and Della drove the twenty miles to Walmart and he bought a prepaid phone, then they returned to his truck and he called his office. "What's up, Emma?"

"We had a peculiar visitor this morning. He was definitely on a fishing expedition."

"What did he want?" Paul backed out of the parking slot and headed for the exit.

"To talk to you about a baby bottle."

The one in Della's fridge? Code for the Baby Killer? Paul couldn't tell Emma that. "Did he leave a number? Anything?"

"He wouldn't. Said he'd call you back at eleven o'clock tomorrow."

It was a trap. Paul knew it. "What'd he look like?"

"Just a normal guy. Kind of thin, short brown hair. He had on sunglasses, so I couldn't see his eyes. Five-ten or so, I guess. Maybe 180 pounds—big biceps and blue shoes."

A chill crawled up Paul's back. "Blue shoes?"

"Yeah. Weird because they weren't navy blue. They were lighter and almost neon. You don't often see a grown man wearing neon-blue shoes. In fact, I've never seen a grown man wearing neon-blue aquatic shoes away from the water."

Just like the man mowing the lawn. Della's stalker. "Call Detective Cray and get with a sketch artist. Let's get a visual on this guy."

"You think he's your man?"

"Sounds like it. It's either him or someone close to him."

"I wish I'd known that when he was in here. Conking Della in the head...I'd have wiped the floor with him."

Emma might have. She was a big woman, and a black belt.

No one messed with her. "I wish you had." The guy had done worse than conk Della, but for some reason that ranked higher on Emma's list of objections than him bombing Della's garage and trying to bomb Paul's SUV.

"I'll phone Cray. Don't you even think about coming here tomorrow to take that call. The detective can work out something."

"I won't." Paul had expected some move to flush them out—just not this one to his office. He figured the stalker's move would come through Lost, Inc. "Later."

"Can I reach you at this number?"

"No, Emma. Sorry."

"No problem, boss. But while I have, you, I have a couple questions."

"Shoot."

She ran through her questions on some of their current cases, and Paul answered them, then ended the call.

"What's happened?" Della looked over at him.

"Mr. Blue Shoes showed up at Vet Net." He passed the phone. "Yank the—"

"Battery," she finished, extracting it and putting the back cover back on the phone. Removing the battery was the ideal way to prevent anyone from tracking them. "You're kidding about Blue Shoes, right? Why would he show up at Vet Net?"

"Not kidding, and no idea." Heading north, Paul checked the rearview. No one was following them.

"We need to let Madison know—but not with this phone." Della lifted it.

"Put the battery back in."

"You're not calling—"

"No."

She replaced the battery and handed him the phone. He dialed.

"Florida Vet Net. This is Emma. How may I help you?"

"Have the office swept for listening devices."

"On it, boss."

"Did Blue Shoes go anywhere else other than the reception area?"

"Restroom, before we talked."

A cold chill swept through Paul's chest, set the roof of his mouth to tingling. "Evacuate the building immediately and then do a thorough sweep. I'll call in an hour to see if you've got an all clear."

"Yes, sir."

Paul disconnected, passed the phone to Della.

She took out the battery. "You think he's planted explosives in your office?"

"I don't know. But I wouldn't be surprised. Would you?"

"No." She squeezed her eyes shut. "We really do need to let Madison know about this."

Paul braked to a stop, turned around and headed back to the store for another phone. "Yeah, we do." This time, he'd buy a couple of spares.

He entered the motel room, toed off the neon-blue shoes and sat down in the bedside chair. Emma had gotten a good look at his shoes. He'd seen to that. And by now, she'd no doubt contacted Paul Mason, who had no doubt told Della, and they had notified Detective Cray. He smiled at the ceiling. Likely they'd talk his visit to Florida Vet Net to death—at least until… *Boom!*

He heard the explosion in his mind. Eager anticipation slithered through his chest. Paul Mason would be devastated that his bleeding-heart organization lay in ruin. It was unfortunate that he wouldn't be in ruin with it. A few months rebuilding, some cash he could well afford to lose—the loss would be no big deal. But killing Emma? The guilt for her death Mason would carry for a long, long time. Likely until he drew his last breath.

Too bad it wasn't Della, but all in good time. Mason had pulled the disappearing act, and until he discovered where

Della was stashed, he had to compromise. No way would Mason take her to his ranch. For now, Emma would do.

He snagged a cold drink from the little fridge and popped the top. He'd done a lot of investigating on Paul Mason. No dirt, not that he couldn't manufacture some if the need arose. Mason was a good guy by all accounts, but hooking up with Della…he'd sealed his fate.

Drinking down a long swallow that cooled the throat, he belched. Della would beg, plead and cry. Not that it would make any difference. He opened the closet doors, peered deep into the closet to the photos taped to the back wall. Photos of Della smiling. Della in her wedding gown, in her uniform. Della holding Danny. Della, Della, Della.

She wasn't a fool, but she was not wise enough to battle him and win.

Rage boiled in his stomach. In so many photos she looked content and happy. Outrageous. She had no right to be happy. None. Seeing her smile fed his fury. The desire to destroy her burned strong.

He stood facing the closet, squeezed his hands into fists at his sides and shut his eyes tight, struggling and fighting the temptation to destroy anything and everything in reach. The temptation nearly buckled him, nearly sliced him in two.

Do it. Cut them. Do it.

He reached to the desktop where he'd placed a host of personal items. His knife lay there beside its sheath, its silver blade gleaming.

Cut them. Cut them. Cut them…

The desire burned like wildfire in his belly. He reached for the knife…and stopped. He couldn't do it. He needed those photographs.

But he didn't need them intact.

He opened his eyes, grabbed the knife and slashed out her perfect mouth, then her perfect eyes and then his. Danny's eyes. Accusing eyes. Eyes filled with blame and disappointment. Eyes that knew the truth.

Frantically, he sliced and carved until all their eyes were gone and they could no longer see. He backed out of the closet and studied his work, his body drenched in sweat, blood pounding through his veins.

Better. Much better.

The disfigured photos would lay blame at the perfect door....

Paul removed the battery from a throwaway phone and looked across the kitchen at Della. Her hair was pulled back and banded, and her face freshly scrubbed. In loose jeans and a T-shirt, she looked so carefree and amazingly serene. His heart sank. Boy, did he hate to mess that up! "Della?"

At the sink, she rinsed a metal mixing bowl and looked back at him. "Yeah?"

"That was Madison on the phone."

She stiffened, leaned into the counter and stopped still, then waited.

"Cray called in Beech. His bomb squad found two explosive devices at Florida Vet Net. They carry the same signature as the one that detonated in your garage. No trip wires, though. Both were on timers. They were set to explode at twelve-eighteen. Mrs. Renault says twelve-eighteen is significant to you."

She paled. The metal bowl slipped from her fingers and clanged in the sink.

"Della?" He walked around the table and over to her. "Why is it significant?"

A shield slid down over her face, removing all expression, and she hid behind it. "That's the time of Danny's death."

She didn't move. Didn't blink.

"Are you okay?"

Stiffening, she straightened her shoulders and reached for the bowl. Her hands were shaking. She was shaking all over. "Nobody was hurt, right?"

Paul wanted to take her in his arms and make the hurt go away, but right now that wasn't what she needed. She needed normalcy. "No, nobody was hurt." He handed her a fresh dish-cloth. Began clearing the table. "Emma's pretty ticked. She's threatening to go on a one-woman crusade to find Mr. Blue Shoes and cook his goose. Mrs. Renault is having a word with her now." They both knew what that meant—ear blistering, in progress. None of them could afford the luxury of anger. They had to remain calm, collected, to win.

She dried the metal bowl. "Maybe she should let her. I've seen Emma in action at a martial arts exhibition. She's pretty formidable."

She was regaining her balance. His own was slipping, and an odd warning took root. "Something's not right in this."

"No, it's not." She put the bowl into the lower cabinet and wiped her hands on the dish towel. "He's a professional and this isn't just a sloppy error. It's a deliberate diversion."

"Astute as always." He popped the leftovers into the fridge and closed the door. "Can you pin down anything specific?"

"Why would he tie up the bomb squad unless—" She gasped. "He never meant for those bombs to detonate. He wanted me to know the time. He wanted me to feel guilty for something else."

"A second set of bombs?"

"Call Beech."

The warning signaled stronger. Paul shoved the battery into a phone and dialed, and when Beech answered, Paul explained their suspicions, then added, "Check Vet Net again and then check Lost, Inc. He's playing us, Beech. You watch your back."

Paul ended the call and removed the battery.

Della tapped her thigh, signaling Jake to come to her. He didn't hesitate. No surprise there. She spoiled him rotten. Bending, she stroked his scruff. Her hand wasn't shaking as badly. A streak of jealousy shot through Paul. Playing second fiddle to an ex was bad, but to his own dog? He stifled a groan. Why not him? Why Jake?

Get your nose back into joint and think—see through her eyes. Jake won't turn on her. Dogs are notoriously loyal. Paul could. Of course he wouldn't, but after Jeff, she couldn't know that unequivocally. Jake was safe. Dogs don't cast blame and they don't leave.

A spark of encouragement ignited in him. That first step was the hardest. A leap. From there, it would just take patience and baby steps to get from Jake to him.

But what if she took those steps? He could turn on her. Not literally but figuratively. Faith was extremely significant to him, and Della was neck-deep in a spiritual crisis from which she might or might not recover. Losing a child. Feeling responsible—rightly or wrongly—for that loss. It impacted her deeply every day of her life in every way, including her faith. How could he not worry about it?

"Well?" Della prodded him.

"Beech is checking the buildings. He'll let us know what he finds."

She tilted her head, studied him. "What's wrong?"

How could he answer that? If he admitted he was experiencing his own faith crisis? Surely God wouldn't put love for her in his heart unless it was right.

But he'd seen too many "right" relationships crash and burn to have any confidence that theirs was immune.

"Paul?" She stood up and asked again, "What's wrong?"

"Nothing." He grabbed a sponge and wiped down the table. "I'm fine."

"You're fine."

That he'd used the one word he found most objectionable hit him. "I mean—"

Della laughed hard and hugged him, planted a kiss on his cheek. "I can't believe you said that."

"Neither can I." He circled her with his arms. "But if this is my reward, I'll say it often."

Jake barked and Warny cleared his throat.

Della backed out of Paul's arms. "Warny."

His face turned red. "I need some chocolate sauce for my ice cream."

The man's timing couldn't have been worse. Another ten seconds and they'd have been kissing. Kissing. Disappointment rammed through him.

Wordlessly, Paul went to the fridge and got the sauce.

NINE

Water rippled down the stream.

To the soothing sounds of it, Della sat down on the sun-warmed blanket and lifted containers of food from an old wicker basket she'd found in the ranch house storage room. "I feel guilty," she told Paul, who dropped down beside her.

"Why?"

"It's Sunday." She shoved back her hair. "If not for me, you'd be at church."

"Going to church right now isn't safe for us or for the others there." He passed her a napkin, then poured two glasses of tea from a stainless thermos. "Especially not after I blew off that phone meeting yesterday with Mr. Blue Shoes. Beech never found any other devices at Vet Net, but your stalker's got to be looking for some way to get revenge."

"Probably. But the church would be a bad place to do it."

"More insulting maybe, which is why Cray and Beech are making sure there are no surprises during the service." Paul took a sip of tea and glanced over at the water. "There'll be plenty of time for us to go to church together."

Clearly, he was testing the waters on that. He did frequently, inviting her to attend with him, but she always politely refused. Sometimes they met afterward for lunch, sometimes not. Since he, too, was acknowledging the shift in their relationship, it was only right to set him straight. "I can't do that, Paul."

"Can't do what?" He cranked back his neck so the sun shone on his face.

Deliberately avoiding making eye contact with her was what he was doing. She staved off a frown. "Go to church."

"Of course you can." He reached into the basket and pulled out a container of potato salad. "Anyone can."

"I can't, not without being a hypocrite."

He passed her a glass. "Your call, of course, and I respect your decision. That goes without saying. But…"

"You don't understand."

"Not really, no." He smiled. "I guess I don't know as much as I thought I did about where your head is on things."

"You know plenty." Again he'd asked and not demanded. She loved that about him. He didn't want to judge her, only to understand her. Admiring that, she said, "When what happened, well, happened with Danny and Jeff, my son and my marriage weren't the only casualties. You know that better than anyone except me."

He nodded, waited.

She liked that, too. His patience in giving her time to think and work through what she wanted to say and the way she wanted to say it. "I stopped believing in justice, except for that we make and choose to embrace ourselves, and in God." She took a sip of her drink. "You won't understand this, but—"

"I'll really try, Della. You have my word on that."

Such a good man. "I know you will. It's one of many things I love about you."

The look in his eyes turned tender.

That was another thing. Mentally shaking herself, she refocused. "The God I believed in would have protected my child and me. He didn't. So He can't be there." She was half tempted to say He might exist because He'd provided her with a surrogate family and Paul, but she didn't. That would create false hope in him on something she'd considered, not adopted.

Paul toed off his shoes and crossed his legs, sitting Indian-style. "But God didn't kill Danny or walk out on you. Dawson and Jeff did. They're mere men—and Dawson was unbalanced."

"In my heart, I know that, but my head says that's all the more reason God should have stepped in and protected us, including Dawson. Yet He didn't. He didn't, and my son is dead." Guilt washed through her like water rushing over the small rocks in the stream. Her throat went tight, and she sought refuge in reciting the poem in her head. *Mother, do not weep. Do not despair. Do not regret. The child now absent from your loving arms rests in arms more loving. Strong arms where no tears are shed, no sadness or struggles are borne, no illness suffered and no pain endured. Wise arms that heal and protect, foster contentment and abundant joy. Be at peace, Mother. Your child is happy, safe and content. Your child is embraced in unconditional love.*

"Della, are you still blaming yourself for Danny?"

The refuge didn't come. She shook, sloshing tea against the sides of her glass. "If he were your son, wouldn't you?"

Paul hesitated, pain twisted on his face. "Yeah, I would. I did. It wasn't right or fair or just, but when Maggie got hurt, I felt like it was my fault." He shrugged, scanned the trees. "I should have protected her."

"So you know exactly how I feel."

"Maybe not exactly, but close. I've always been kind of a parent to Maggie."

That encouraged Della to open up more, to say things she'd only thought about in the dark of night. "If I'd been home and not off fighting a war, I would have gotten the mail that day. I'd be dead, and Danny would be alive." Hearing herself saying that aloud had sharp pains twisting in her stomach and shooting through her chest, and the tears she'd blocked and buried and shielded herself against for three long years gushed forth. She couldn't stop them. "Jeff was right, Paul. So was Dawson." *Baby killer.* "Danny is dead and it's my fault because I wasn't there to protect him." She wept, and when Paul pulled her into his arms and circled her, rocking back and forth with her head buried at his shoulder, she sobbed and sobbed.

And she kept on sobbing until she had nothing left. Not another tear.

Wrung dry, she let out a shuddery sigh and sank against him.

"I was there and couldn't protect Maggie. I get it. But I wasn't to blame, and you're not, either, Della." He pulled back, dabbed at her wet face with a paper napkin in gentle strokes. "I don't know why God didn't stop Dawson or Jeff any more than I know why He hasn't stopped Gary Crawford. I wish I did. I've begged and pleaded for understanding and acceptance."

"How can you keep believing, then?" She didn't get it—and only now realized she really wanted to get it.

"Because He said we'd go through trials, not that we wouldn't, and He'd be there with us. It's hard, but I hang on to that."

She sniffed, rested her head against his chest, felt his heartbeat strong and steady against her ear. "In a way, I guess He has been. I lost my family but I've had you and Miss Addie and the people at work. I felt alone—I thought I had to be to survive—but I wasn't really. What's happened with this stalker and setup has proven that, the way everyone's stepped up to help me. I'm not alone and haven't been since our first phone conversation." Her eyes blurred. "Thank you for that, Paul."

"You've done the same for me." He stroked her hair. "You'll always have me. That's a promise."

She risked looking up at him expecting a smile. There wasn't one. Instead his eyes shone overly bright, serious and full of unwavering promise. He'd trudged through the tear storm with her. And so moved that he would, so tender and touched, she couldn't resist. Raising her arms, she nudged his head lower and pressed her lips to his. He welcomed her, but not with the tender and friendly kiss he had shown her in the past. No. No gentle kiss, this. This kiss was unfettered, raw emotion expressed openly, unabashedly and without apology. This kiss was not the kiss of a friend, but of a man invested in a woman. A man both knowing and acknowledging the pain and emptiness of loneliness and longing, seeking reassurance, offering it, yearning to leave no doubt in either of them that they were not alone anymore. They had each other, and that was more than enough.

Startled by sheer intensity, they sank deeper, then deeper still into each other's arms, into the life-affirming sensation of mattering and being accepted and significant to each other, and when Paul finally parted their lips, breaking the kiss, they stared deeply into each other's eyes, shaken by all that kiss had conjured and all that had transpired between them.

Della opened her mouth. "That was even better than I dreamed."

He smiled. "You dreamed about me kissing you?"

"Um, actually, I kissed you." She started to keep quiet and leave it at that but couldn't. Not after the connection she'd just experienced. "Thoughts of us kissing like that is all that has gotten me through a lot of nights."

His eyes warmed, twinkled with that special look he reserved just for her. "I've dreamed about you, too, Della."

"No, you haven't." She smiled, squeezed his arm. "You don't have to say that just because I did."

"I wasn't."

She stilled. Fear and doubt latched on to her and sank in deep, and she sobered. "Oh, no." *Fool! Fool! Fool!* "Paul, what have we done?"

"What do you mean?" He went serious. "Della, you look terrified. I'm the same guy I've always—"

"I am terrified." Tears she thought she didn't have to cry gathered on her lashes. "Everything's changed. What was I thinking? Why didn't I think?" Her fingers curled at his shoulder, grasping bits of his soft shirt.

"Think about what?"

Her heart cracked in two. "You'll leave me just like you've left the others."

"What are you talking about?"

"You don't get serious. A woman gets serious about you, and you run." She grabbed his arms. "What am I going to do without you?"

He laughed. Pulled her into his arms and held her head against his chest. His heart beat hard and fast against her ear.

That angered her. "I guess that kiss meant a whole lot more to me than you. How can you laugh at me about this?"

"Because it is what it is."

"What is what it is?"

"You have nothing to fear." He kissed her forehead. "I don't run."

She stilled. Her anger drained. She looked up at the underside of his chin. "I've seen you do it, Paul Mason."

"No, you really haven't. You thought you had, but what you've seen is me waiting for you to get to a point where you'd really let me into your life. I'm crazy about you. I have been since the first time we talked on the phone. But you were wounded and needed to heal. I didn't mean for that kiss to happen yet. It just did. But I won't apologize for it. It was the most amazing kiss I've had in my life."

"Really?" When he nodded, she took a full minute to let that sink in. Then another. Then a third. And finally she confessed, "For me, too."

"Then let's just leave it alone for now. You trust me. I trust you. It will all work out exactly as it's supposed to work out. Let's just enjoy our picnic and not think for a while. Does that sound okay?"

She smiled. "It sounds better than okay." He'd said and meant it. He didn't intend to run. But Paul Mason was a man of habit, and running was a long-standing bad habit.

And everyone with sense knew that bad habits were hardest to break.

* * *

Dusk settled in on the ranch.

Della and Paul sat on the front porch with a huge metal bowl on the floor between them. A burlap sack of beans sat beside it, and it was about two-thirds empty. A smaller bowl was used for the tips being discarded. Jake had given up begging an hour ago and lay sprawled out near Della's chair.

She snapped a bean and tossed it into the big bowl. "Today's been a good day."

"For me, too. One of the best I've had at home in... One of the best I've had at home."

Her heart fluttered. Gratitude filled it that she'd been part of what had made a good day for him. He deserved many good days. More. He deserved everything good life had to offer.

It'd been a pleasant two hours since Warny had returned from church and lunch in town with the bag of beans and announced his fingers didn't work well enough anymore to snap them. "I wish Madison would get some news. I love being here, but I feel awful, ousting you from your home." He'd spent nights in the barn with Warny, who apparently snored loud enough to wake the dead.

"I like you being here." Paul kept snapping. The beans hit the metal bowl steadily. *Ping. Ping. Ping.*

His phone rang—a throwaway he used to communicate with Madison on her throwaway. He answered it. "Hey."

Paul whispered it was Madison, spoke briefly, then ended the call and looked at Della. "Detective Cray wants you to call him about Jeff."

She paused in snapping a bean. "What about him?"

"The woman he's been seeing reported him missing. Cray told her he'd talked with Jeff, but the woman says he couldn't have. Jeff hasn't been seen or heard from in weeks."

Della frowned. "But Cray did talk with him. He told you so himself. And Jeff told Cray the woman had passed him the message to call Cray."

"Well, she's changing her tune now."

Della snapped a bean, then another. "If Cray said he talked to her and Jeff, then surely he did."

"Della, his fiancée hasn't seen him—"

"Fiancée?" The word cut through her like a hot knife.

Paul nodded. "Didn't I tell you that? Cray said the woman's planning a Christmas wedding. I thought I'd told you."

"No. I would have remembered that." Della swallowed hard.

"I'm sorry. With your injury and everything, I guess… I'm sorry." He dropped his gaze to the bean bowl. "I can see this has hit you hard." Paul pulled away visually, in his distant tone and expression.

Her heart rebelled. He thought she still loved Jeff. "It's not a problem," she quickly added. From the uncertainty in Paul's eyes, maybe too quickly. Jeff's remarrying did bother her, but not for the reason Paul suspected.

Paul studied her for signs that she'd just given him a *fine* without saying *fine*. "Do you need a few minutes before calling Cray?"

Definitely gauging her reaction in a big way. After the kisses they'd shared, as close as they'd become, she fully understood that. "No, go ahead."

"You sure?" He dropped a bean into the bowl. "It's okay to be rattled about your ex remarrying, you know."

She gave him a smile—and it was genuine. "If I were rattled, it would be okay, but I'm not."

"Something is off. If it's not that, then what is it?"

"Madison told you Jeff hasn't been seen in Tennessee for weeks. His fiancée hasn't seen him, and now she's reported him missing. Cray said Jeff told him he'd been at his cabin and out of touch. There's a hole in that story."

"Why?" Easier now, he started snapping beans again. "A lot of mountain cabins don't have phones."

"Jeff's never owned a cabin. He could have bought one, but he hates being away from town. He's definitely not a tree-loving kind of guy, which is why we need to verify his actual location at the time he and Cray spoke."

Paul's expression turned dark. "Surely Cray ran a check on that. Surely—"

"If you're confident, then we can forget it." She snapped a bean, tossed it in the bowl.

"Not when you're at risk." Paul pulled out a second throw-away phone and dialed. "But the cabin could belong to his fiancée."

"It could." Della bent to pull more beans out of the sack. "Ask that, too."

Paul paused a long minute, then said, "Cray, it's Mason. When you spoke to Jeff Jackson, where did he say he was?"

He mouthed to Della, "Tennessee." He tilted the phone to speak into it. "Did you verify ownership of the cabin he was supposedly in?" A pause, then, "I see."

"They haven't checked." Della frowned. "Now ask the question," she whispered to Paul.

"I don't know if it's important. It depends." Another pause, and then Paul added, "When you two talked, he said he was calling from Tennessee. But where was he actually at the time?" Again, Paul paused, and his expression turned thunderous. "Find out."

The blood drained from Della's face, and the warm evening suddenly turned chilly. Jeff could have been anywhere. Could be anywhere. Cray hadn't checked on the cabin or verified the call location.

Jeff could be her stalker.

They finished snapping the beans. Cooked and ate dinner. They played Monopoly with Warny until after one in the morning. And still the detective hadn't called back.

Paul was outraged. Della seemed edgy but not out of sorts about Jeff remarrying. Could Paul trust that? Did he dare? How could she not hold it against him that he hadn't told her right away? His stomach hollowed.

Warny scooted back from the kitchen table. "Well, that's it for me."

"I guess so. You wiped us both out." Paul forced a smile. "How'd you get so smart on land deals?"

He grunted. "You don't live as long as I have without picking up a tip or two." He grunted and groaned, stiff after sitting so long, then ambled toward the back door, pausing to scan the monitors. "Night, Miss Della. See you directly, Paul," Warny said, then went on outside to the barn.

Della put the top back on the Monopoly game box. "He's a shrewd player."

Paul rinsed their glasses at the sink, then put them in the dishwasher. "He's just plain shrewd. Most people miss that about him."

"Appearances can be deceptive." She tiptoed, stretching to put the game back on the top shelf in the little hallway closet. "Guess I'll see you in the morning."

"Della, wait." Paul dried his hands and then set the dish towel on the counter. "I know it's late, but if we don't talk about this, I'll be up all night wondering."

"What?" She walked back into the kitchen and stopped next to the stove.

Paul turned to face her, nearly brushing their knees. "Are you really okay with Jeff remarrying?"

"Yeah, I really am." She shrugged. "It kind of surprised me, and I thought it would hurt, but it just doesn't. I guess because he wasn't the man I thought he was. You know what I mean. We all disappoint each other sometimes, but what he did...well, he just wasn't the man I believed him to be, and I don't think the man he really is was right for me. I know he can't be trusted."

"I'm glad to hear that—not that he can't be trusted, but that you're not upset about him getting married." He swayed his focus from the oven clock back to her and admitted the truth. "I was worried."

He had been. It'd been evident since he'd told her on the porch, though she'd half attributed that to Cray's not calling back and the tension getting to him. The tension sure had gotten to her. "Why?"

Paul wrapped his arms across his chest as if preparing to hold in hurt. Shielding himself. Seeing that got to her. Not being sure he'd ever been loved got to her. "Talk to me, Paul."

"The truth is, having you here…" He stopped short, sighed. "I don't want to be just your friend. I want more."

She'd known that from his kiss. Recalling it left her slightly dazed even now. She worried her lip. "You're an amazing man, and if I could give you more, I'd do it. It'd be a privilege and an honor."

"You don't owe me, Della."

"I do, but that's not why. Because you really do awe me, Paul. Words are cheap. But you show you care through actions. You always have. I love that about you. The problem is, I don't know that I have more to give." She blinked hard, pressed a hand to her chest. "My heart can't survive another shatter. I can't take another shatter. I lost everything. You know that."

"You still feel you have nothing left to lose?"

How did she answer that? *Honestly?* Did she dare? "No, not really. This is hard." She grabbed the back of a chair, squeezed. "I have something. With you, I have something special. And I treasure it. But, okay, say we're more than friends. What if it doesn't work? What happens to us then? What's left for either of us?"

"I don't know."

"Me, either, but I know I don't want to find out. Do you?"

He ignored her question and asked his own. "So between the picnic at the creek and now, you've thought about us, and you're not interested in me? As more than friends, I mean."

Harder still. Much harder. "I can't say that."

"Thank goodness." He stepped closer, clasped her arms. "Look, I know you're scared. Truthfully, I am, too. All my life, I've made myself not need anything from anyone. Not even Maggie. I love her, but I couldn't need her. But you—"

"You need me?"

"Yeah, I do," he reluctantly admitted. "I told you that you rescued me."

Paul needed her. *Her.* After being shunned, that must have been hard to admit. So hard to realize and accept. "But—"

He placed his fingertips over her mouth, looked deeply into her eyes. "With everything going on, I know now's not the best time. But this is life, you know? Something's always going on."

"Hopefully not the kind of things we've had happening, Paul."

He conceded that with a nod. "I didn't choose now to feel all I do for you. God did. His timing's perfect. I trust that, and I trust you."

She wanted to kiss him again. To lose herself in his arms and forget everything but the two of them. Yet it wouldn't be fair. Not with their challenges and with the issues between them remaining unchanged. Their differences might be fine today, but what about tomorrow, next week or next year?

"Don't worry, Della. I'm not pushing. I just wanted you to know that to me you're more than a friend." He stroked her arm. "I believe in us and I trust things will work out."

"You honestly believe that?"

"I do, yes." He let her see the truth in his eyes. "You're a brave woman. Far too brave not to make peace with caring for me, with yourself and maybe even with God."

"That matters a great deal to you." What if she didn't? He'd be disappointed, resentful. That would create tension, and how long would it take for that to break their bond?

Longer than three years. It hadn't broken it yet. He hadn't been judgmental or disappointed or resentful, either.

He lowered his voice. "You matter to me, Della. You've always mattered, and you always will."

This wasn't a declaration of love. It was a declaration of being open to love. Could she do that? He thought she was brave, but was she that brave? He had been. Admitting he needed her when he'd trained his whole life to need nothing. If he could do that for her, she could try to be brave for him.

Paul kissed her, then kissed her again, rubbing gentle circles on her back.

She opened her mouth to speak, though she had no idea what she intended to say; she couldn't pull her thoughts together. She was feeling way too much.

He pressed his fingertips to her lips. "No, just know you matter to me, and I don't expect you to be anything other than yourself."

An alien feeling swarmed her. Deep inside, the flare of hope grew to a flame and burned strong, shooting sparks that spread through her body and limbs, so pure her skin tingled. Looking into his eyes, she pegged the sensation. It was caring. She cared, and if only to herself, she admitted the truth. Not feeling hollow felt good.

So good. For such a long time, she'd felt empty and dead inside. A lump in her chest rose to her throat. The back of her nose stung, and her eyes burned. Healing was not painless. It came through hope and caring. It came through opening old wounds, cleansing them. It came through compassion for oneself as well as others, and it came through—

One of Paul's phones rang.

Neither of them appreciated the interruption. He answered, "Yes?"

He listened for a long moment, mouthed to Della, "Warny." Della smiled. "Keeping my reputation intact."

Paul laughed. "I'm on my way."

"Night." Della went upstairs, torn between smiling and frowning. She cared. The fact scared her to death, but she felt...alive. She waited for the guilt to swamp her. Twinges of it tried, but something else proved stronger. Fearful of discovering what it was, she rounded the corner at the head of the stairs and went into her room, then closed the door and it hit her that they still hadn't heard back from Cray.

The detective could have gotten that information on Jeff in fifteen minutes—an hour at most. So why hadn't he called back?

Maybe he had gotten detained or sidetracked. Maybe he was waiting for feedback from someone in Tennessee. Or maybe he didn't want to deliver bad news in the middle of the night.

She showered and got into bed, then did something she hadn't done in a long time. She folded her hands and began to pray, tentatively. "I'm not sure if You're there and listening, but I am open to the possibility. If You are, and You wouldn't mind, I'd appreciate Your help keeping everyone You've put in my path safe. I don't want anyone else I care about getting hurt because of me."

A wealth of sadness flooded her. The Bible said God would never give anyone more to deal with than he or she could handle. Truthfully, she'd pretty much maxed out. Maybe He thought she could stand more, but she knew she'd reached her limit. Maybe He'd keep that in mind and protect her friends.

Della bit her lip, torn and struggling with her thoughts and her feelings for Paul—her gratitude that he was in her life. Without him, she'd be upset about Jeff's getting married again. But Paul helped her see things differently, even to see Jeff through compassionate eyes.

Closing her eyes, she continued. "I'm not that good or holy. But I am grateful, and I want You to know that." Feeling alone had been really hard, and caring could hurt. She didn't want to hurt, but she didn't want to feel dead inside anymore, either. Not wanting to crawl into a hole and die wasn't truly living. And Della wanted to live.

I want to heal. Fear slithered through her. Opening herself up for more pain, more disappointment, more despair. Had she lost her mind? Healing meant living a full life. It meant pain. It meant forgetting....

The strongest sense came over her, the feeling to pay attention. Forgetting. That's what she'd been thinking about. Dawson had caused her more pain than she thought anyone could bear and survive, killing her son. She hadn't forgotten Dawson, but she had forgiven him. He was sick.

But she hadn't forgiven herself. Did she deserve forgiving?

She didn't. Her son, her responsibility. She'd failed. But what about grace? With the awful things people did, God could still forgive them. Her act hadn't been intentional. She'd gladly trade her life for his. Forgiveness, anyway—grace—that was the only hope for her. But she didn't deserve it. Didn't trust it.

Wait. Grace is grace. It can't be earned. No one deserves it.

She buried her nose in her pillow, let the darkness settle over her. The mind twisted things, made them easier to bear. But it didn't really change anything. The guilt and blame remained—earned and warranted or not.

Or did it?

Grace. Choice. She could *choose* to forgive herself. She could have done so at any time in the past three years. But she hadn't. What kind of a person chose pain? Chose three long years of agony?

She had chosen the perimeters of her life. What she deserved and didn't, what she was worthy to experience and too unworthy to experience. The absence of anything and everything but work. The lack of things, and even simple pleasures like laughter, like fun. She'd treated herself with far less mercy and compassion than she would a stranger. She hadn't trusted herself not to forget. To go on living a full life and not forget Danny and Jeff. Self-imposed punishment for crimes she hadn't committed. Why hadn't she seen that? Why?

It was time to let go of the pain and choose forgiveness. Time to give herself permission to heal and to attempt to do it and forgive herself. God was merciful. He'd known how much she'd suffered, how deeply. And surely He would agree, she'd suffered enough.

She'd try. She'd really try.

She closed her eyes and relaxed, let her mind be at peace.

Warmth flooded her. It was familiar and had been gone far too long.

Unconditional love.

TEN

"What are you doing?"

Paul stepped into the kitchen, wearing jeans and a blue-and-gray flannel shirt. He smelled of soap from the shower.

"Cooking." Della stirred a pot of spaghetti sauce, tapped the spoon against the edge of the pot, set it in a saucer and then looked at Paul. He appeared thunderstruck.

"But you hate cooking."

"Well, that's not actually true. I used to love it. What I hated was eating alone and not having anyone to cook for, so I quit."

"Oh." He processed that and still seemed unsure of what to do with it. "It smells good."

She smiled; she couldn't help herself. "You'll love it."

He smiled back, settling into the idea. "I, um, need to run out to the creek."

"Want me to ride along?"

"Not this time." He frowned. "Something's glinting on the monitor, reflecting sun, and it shouldn't be. I'm going to see what it is. Could be a piece of foil or something blown by the wind."

"There is no wind. It's still as glass out there." She stirred the sauce. "Let me come with you, just in case you need backup."

"Warny's riding backup. You keep an eye on the monitor. The alarm has to be down with us out there. Otherwise, it'll go off nonstop."

"But Warny can't see a thing, Paul." Worry flooded her voice. She loved the endearing recluse, but he was bat-blind.

"He'll wear his glasses." Paul pressed a quick kiss to her temple. "Just watch the monitors and don't come out there."

"But—"

"Promise me, Della. You'd be in a goldfish bowl. I can't have that." He clasped her shoulder. "I'm probably overreacting, but considering what all's happened, I need to check to put my mind at ease."

She nodded. "Be careful." It could be nothing. But once again it didn't feel like nothing. It felt like a whole lot of something.

He walked to the back door. "Warny's armed."

Considering his *shoot first, ask questions later* attitude, staying put was wise advice. "Understood."

Paul left the house. Warny sat waiting, astride Thunder and holding the reins on a beautiful black beast that had to be seventeen hands high. His coat gleamed in the sun. Paul stroked its neck and then mounted the horse, told Jake through the glass door, "Guard," and then rode off.

Jake danced around, his nails clicking on the tile floor. He was itching to go but didn't whine to be let out. Yet if something was wrong out there, Jake could be needed. She was fine. The alarm was off, but she was safe in the house. Della opened the back door and told Jake, "Go with him, boy," then thrust a hand toward Paul.

The dog didn't have to be told twice. He ran full out.

Della watched until she couldn't see them anymore and then entered the monitor room. Scanning quickly, she found the stream and saw the glinting object. It was on the ground near where they'd had their picnic on Sunday.

Paul spotted Jake running toward him and frowned. Della had sent him. There was no way Jake would have left her side otherwise. Irritated, he spurred the horse to the stream, then searched for the tree he'd used to mark the location of the glinting object. Stubborn woman, but one with instincts he respected. She'd be alert, making sure that while the alarm was down, she kept a sharp eye out.

He adjusted his hat to block the sun. She'd be glued to the monitors, watching him and his back. In the kitchen cooking. Della. He couldn't get over that. He'd thought she hated it, but it was eating alone, having no one to share her meals. She must have loved cooking a lot at one time, or it wouldn't be such a big deal to her that she totally avoided her kitchen.

Approaching the tree, he slowed his horse. A panting Jake caught up, nose to the ground, he sniffed and followed a straight path to the shiny object. Paul dismounted and looked into the camera, signaled Della with an okay sign.

Jake plopped down beside it. What it was, Paul couldn't yet see. He approached and stopped. His blood ran cold.

Warny rode up. "What is it, son?"

Paul looked back at him. "A baby bottle."

And on it written in red: *D.B.D.*

"That sure didn't blow in here by itself."

Paul's stomach clenched. "No, it didn't." He scanned the woods, the stream. Pulled a ziplock bag out of his pocket and captured the bottle, then put it near Jake's nose. "Find it, boy."

Thunder snorted, and Warny asked, "What does it mean?"

It felt like Crawford's work. His arrogance. Paul turned to Warny. "It means Della's stalker knows she's at the ranch."

The dog was tracking his scent.

Standing in the four-wheeler, he adjusted the binoculars and picked up Mason on horseback, following the dog's lead. He'd found the bottle—a little faster than expected. The man was good, and definitely watchful. Where was the old man?

He panned the binoculars and spotted him riding back toward the ranch house. Moving slow for a man expecting trouble there. He studied the horse's gait. It was the horse. Not negligence.

Interesting. So Della was alone in the house, and her guard was limping back to her while her hero tracked her soon-to-be killer. He smiled.

Cray hadn't gotten that phone call in to them. He said he had, but that they were here proved he hadn't. He'd lied. *Excellent.*

Things were moving along exactly as planned.

He looked back to the dog. Homed in on him, and in a full run, heading right to him.

It was time.

He dropped down into his seat, popped the four-wheeler into gear and took off.

Della watched the monitors. Warny, armed with his shotgun and wearing his glasses, watched her, the doors and the windows. Thunder stood on the lawn tethered to the corner post of the back porch. If anyone approached, he'd whinny and let them know.

Warny paced, clearly worried. "You eyes on in there?"

Eyes on. A military term. Apparently Warny hadn't always been a recluse. "Paul's still not back on the monitors." She scanned and scanned, her nerves strumming, hoping for a glimpse of him or his black beast or Jake.

Another hour passed. Then another. Noon came and went and the day wore on. The house remained silent. No music, no news on the television, no anything that could hamper them from hearing every creak.

Della was thirsty. "Warny, come watch the monitors so I can get us some tea."

He walked into the monitor room and peered from one screen to another. "I don't like it. He's been out of touch too long."

He had. "Me, either," Della admitted.

"Smells like Crawford to me. It surely does."

"Why?"

"He ambushed and nearly killed Paul." He glanced over his shoulder at her. "Betcha didn't know that."

She filled two glasses with sweet tea and ice. "He told me."

"Naw, not the half of it. To him, the attack and everything else is all about Maggie."

Walking back from the kitchen to the monitor room, Della passed Warny a filled glass. "It happened in Utah," she said. "He told me he'd been injured, but that was about all he said about himself." He had said more about Maggie.

"He was unconscious for three days. In ICU a solid week."

Chills swept through Della. "He didn't tell me that."

"Told ya. That's Paul." He frowned. "He took a bad one to the head. It gave him balance problems for months."

"So he was a patient there at the same time as Maggie?"

Warny nodded. "He wasn't hurt as bad, of course, but he was still in the hospital—Maggie was still in ICU—when their folks went back home." Warny rubbed at his neck. "I couldn't believe those two left the kids there in that shape with that monster on the loose."

Neither could she. If it had been Danny, they'd have had to pry her away from him with a crowbar. "You went to Utah." The truth hit Della. "You watched over them." Paul hadn't been alone. God had given him Warny.

"Till I could bring them home with me. Neither one of them was in the best shape to be flying back, but Paul wanted to get back to the ranch. He figured if he could get Maggie home, she'd fare better." He grunted. "I have to say, she did. Paul got her started rescuing animals and that kept her going. Crawford had her scared of her own shadow. She quit the FBI—she was a profiler—and she wanted to lock herself away. But the animals warmed up to her. Some had been abused and even tortured, but they knew they could trust her, and she trusted them. They got my Maggie girl back on an even keel." He blinked hard. "Paul was a good brother. Only real parent she had."

"Isn't he still?"

"You know it." Warny cleared his throat. "Good thing, too, considering my sister is who she is. If it ain't about her or her husband, she ain't interested, and that's the sorry truth. Paul and Maggie always had only each other. Well, and me, but I ain't much."

Special, special man. "That's not so, Warny. You were there for them. Loving them. There's no better gift than that. I think you are more to them than you think."

"Naw. I'm just an old uncle who never got on with his sister. Didn't even know Paul and Maggie until they was grown. Course, I didn't know how their folks treated 'em or I'd have come sooner. That was my fault—the not knowing. But fact is I didn't know and I should've. And that makes me nothing special."

Paul hadn't been loved as a boy. But his uncle loved the man. "You're special to them, and to me. Standing here, putting your life on the line to protect me…" Her eyes blurred. "That's more than special."

Warny shrugged. "Being honest, Miss Della, I think you're a fine woman and my nephew deserves the best. Lord knows, he ain't never had it—tender feelings, I'm talking about. Women have wanted what he could give 'em, even his mama was that way, but you're the first that asks for nothing and just appreciates the man. That makes it a privilege to do what I can to look out for you."

"Because Paul needs looking after?"

"No, ma'am. Because he loves you and I think if you'll scoot out of your own way and let yourself, you'll find out you love him back."

"I do love him," she said before realizing she was speaking.

"Course you do. But now, there's love, and then there's *love*," Warny went on. "It's clear to anyone with eyes you two love each other. I reckon that makes the question whether or not you *love* each other, too. That's something only the two of you can answer and ain't none of this old man's busin— Look! There he is!"

Paul showed up on the monitor, tracking back downstream to where they'd had the picnic. Jake ran alongside him. They cut across the open pasture and headed toward the house.

Relief washed through Della, and her eyes burned. What was wrong with her? She hadn't cried for three years. Then she prayed last night, everything changed and she turned into a virtual waterworks.

She sniffed. "Oh, thank goodness."

Paul came in hot and sweaty, smelling of horse and sunshine. "Everything okay?"

"We're fine," Warny answered before Della could. "No activity."

Della passed him a fresh glass of tea. "You okay?"

"Frustrated. It was him, Della." Paul took a drink of the tea.

"How do you know?" That he knew wasn't in doubt. It showed in every line on his face, in the set of his jaw, the hard expression and outrage in his eyes.

"He left his calling card." He pulled the baby bottle inside the ziplock bag from his pocket.

On its side, she saw the *D.B.D.* Her heart raced, her limbs tingled. "Did you see him?"

"Jake lost his scent in the stream. I got a glimpse of neon blue through the trees. Someone on a four-wheeler. I could hear it but didn't get a clear line of sight."

"Nothing showed up on the monitors. We've been watching nonstop."

"He wasn't on my land." Paul walked back to the kitchen and sat down at the table. "He knew where the field of vision ended."

"Then he's been scoping out the ranch." Warny sat down beside Paul. "Son, I ain't one for running, and you know it. But if Crawford knows the layout of your security, and he knows Miss Della is here—"

She had to go. A hard knot slid from her chest, hollowed her stomach. "I don't think it's Crawford, Warny. I don't think it's Leo Dawson, either."

"Jeff?" Paul asked.

She nodded. "I'm afraid so."

"I ain't too sure, Miss Della."

"It's the only thing that makes sense. If Crawford were out there, he'd have shot you, Paul. That would hurt Maggie far more than doing anything to me."

"Dawson?" Paul refilled his glass from the crockery pitcher on the countertop near the stove.

"There's too much method to this. It just doesn't fit his erratic behavior."

"Well, I hate to say it, but it don't exactly fit Jeff's behavior, either, does it?"

"I don't know, Warny. Who he was, who he is now… I just don't know." She squeezed a slice of lemon into her glass. "But Cray not calling back has me worried. Madison, Jeff… There's only one reason he wouldn't call by now—he can't. And why he can't worries me most."

"She's right about that." Warny nodded to add weight to his claim.

"I know." Paul frowned into his tea.

One of Paul's phones rang. "Madison," he said on answering it.

He listened for a few minutes, then hung up. His eyes had been serious. Now they were sober.

"Who's dead?" Warny asked.

"Not dead but hurt," Paul said, letting his gaze slide to Della. "Cray was attacked last night. He's going to make it, but he was beaten pretty badly."

"Who did it?"

"Unidentified male wearing neon-blue shoes. Cray had run

the call and a property check, Della. Jeff doesn't own a cabin, and the call was relayed from a tower in Panama City."

"Why would a call from Tennessee get routed through Panama City?" Warny asked.

"It didn't. Panama City was first tower to pick up the call. Jeff was in Panama City when he called Cray."

Della shook. She laced her hands in her lap to hide the trembling. "Then I was right. This is Jeff."

"Looks entirely possible."

The same sense of betrayal she'd felt at the airport flooded her, but it didn't sink in and take hold. He'd been revealed. She sat unharmed, and he'd been revealed. "It's time for me to go home."

"What?"

"Miss Della, no."

"Yes." She looked at Paul. "Jeff wants to hurt me. I'm not going to put anyone else in his line of fire. Detective Cray could have been killed. Don't you see? I can't keep letting other people act as shields for me. Not knowing what he's capable of doing. I just can't."

"Della, he's dangerous. You're not alone."

"No, I'm not. But I'm not Maggie, either, Paul. I can't spend what's left of my life always looking over my shoulder. I won't run from him. I just won't. And I won't be the reason he blows up your ranch or barn or hurts the rescue animals."

"Courageous but not in your best interest, Miss Della."

"It's not courageous. If I run or hide or I'm always looking back over my shoulder, I won't ever be able to look ahead. I give in to that, Warny, and I'm already dead."

Paul frowned. "I'm opposed to this."

"Noted." She stroked his face. "Take me home, Paul."

He argued with her the entire time she packed her belongings but got nowhere. What was he going to do? She couldn't just go home and wait for Jeff to attack her, but that's what she planned to do.

Paul kept arguing on the drive back to North Bay, until Madison called and said she needed for them to come into the office at Lost, Inc., and consult.

He'd find reinforcements there who could be more persuasive. Della had dug in her heels and wouldn't budge. She was being noble. Taking all the risks and dangers on herself, pushing him and Warny and Jake, the rescued horses and the ranch, and everyone at Lost, Inc., out of her stalker's range. Her intentions were honorable, but he failed to make her see they were shortsighted, too.

Yet—his chest warmed—Warny had heard her praying. Not for herself, for Paul.

That moved him. Touched him. Warny and Maggie were likely the only two people who ever had prayed for him in his whole life.

That offered him hope. She more than cared about him. Maybe even loved him, though she might not yet realize it. But Della Jackson wouldn't pray to God unless she believed He existed and she wouldn't pray to Him for Paul's protection unless she felt He was capable of granting that protection. He could logically conclude that somehow Della had found her way back to God.

That awed him. For her, for them. So, while worried sick about this stalker—it had to be Jeff—Paul was also nearly overcome with gratitude.

"Why does Madison want to touch base in person?" Della asked. "She said to stay away from here."

"She didn't say."

"You called her and told her what you found by the stream and prodded her to tell you to tell me she wanted to consult." She laid a steady glare on him. "You called in backup to get me to stay put."

Caught red-handed, he had no choice but to confess. "Yes." His face burned.

Della smiled, pecked a kiss to his cheek. "I adore you."

Much, much better than the ear blistering he expected. She was nearly as good at it as Mrs. Renault. Glad to be spared, he smiled back at her. "I adore you, too." He clasped her chin in his hand. "Della, I—"

"I know. You're worried." She pressed her lips to his hand. "Me, too. But it'll work out as it's supposed to, right?"

"It is what it is." He sighed. "But that doesn't give us a license not to do all we can do to be smart about what we do."

"Exactly." She unclicked her seat belt. "Let's go get this done."

Paul frowned. The odds of Madison having any better luck than he'd had were a million to none. Not one. None.

"Ah, good, Della. You're here. Hello, Paul." Mrs. Renault came out from behind her desk and locked the door leading outside. "They're all waiting in the conference room."

"She knows I called," Paul told Mrs. Renault.

"Of course she does. She's stubborn, dear, not stupid." Mrs. Renault's tweed skirt swished against her calves. "Your objections will have to wait, Della. Madison just took a call from the detective. She's got news."

They rushed upstairs and into the conference room. Doc and Jimmy sat in their usual chairs, and Madison sat in hers at the head of the table. "Della. Paul."

"What did Cray say?" Della asked before Paul could.

"Don't bother sitting down," Madison said, gaining her feet. "The clerk at The Shipping Store in Panama City—"

"Sammy," Della said.

Madison nodded. "He got worried after you guys were there. So he's been reviewing the security tapes. He's captured a photo of the woman who shipped the package. Della, she looks just like you."

"Did he send it to you?" Paul asked.

"He refused. I think he's afraid of having to testify. But Mrs. Renault knows the owner and he sent it to her."

Mrs. Renault pulled a photo out of a file and passed it over to Della. "Here you go."

Paul leaned over her shoulder and he and Della studied the photo. "She does look a lot like me."

Madison agreed. "But she's not nearly so interesting as something else in the photo. Look closely."

Paul slowed his scan and saw what Madison meant. Just outside the door, clipping the very edge of the camera's frame, he spotted the toe tips of a pair of shoes. They were neon blue.

"It's him." Surprise streaked through him and he pivoted his gaze to Madison. "He was there, watching."

"Which makes the identity of the woman all the more significant, doesn't it?"

"It does." Paul frowned and asked Madison, "So who is she? Do you know?"

"We do now." Madison looked at Della. "Care to guess?"

Della winced. "The Christmas bride."

Paul groaned. "Jeff's fiancée?"

Mrs. Renault pulled out a second photograph, passed it to Della. "Meet Tamela Baker soon-to-be Jackson."

At first glance, it had to be like Della was looking into a mirror. But with a more serious look, subtle differences became evident. Tamela Baker's eyes were wider set, her mouth fuller, her jaw a touch more square. And Della certainly didn't have a butterfly tattoo on her wrist.

Della snatched up the security camera photo she'd placed on the table and compared them. "The tattoo."

"The tattoo," Madison said, smiling.

Jimmy let out a heartfelt "Whew. I told you he snapped."

"Yes, you did." Della's eyes burned. A tear leaked from her eye.

It startled her coworkers and Madison.

Paul mouthed, *Don't notice.*

She tossed the photo onto the table. "Excuse me." Della rushed from the conference room.

Paul started to go after her.

Mrs. Renault stopped him. "Give her a minute."

"But she's crying," he protested.

"She's healing, Paul."

"It's so time." Madison got misty. "When she comes back, you two return to the ranch. Even if he knows Della is there, it's still safer than anywhere else. We'll get a protection detail out there."

"I'm all for that, but she's insisting on going home to protect everyone else."

Madison pursed her lips. "I agree with her. She can't run. How can she ever have a life if she's busy running all the time? It's like with Maggie. He'll torment her forever, and that's just no kind of life."

"So she makes herself bait?" That was not happening. Paul didn't like the way this was going. "No." Agitated, he didn't bother trying to hide the fact. "Where's Deaver?"

"Proving his loyalty. He's gone to see Talbot and Dayton. It's a fishing expedition to see if he can get anything helpful out of them." Madison wrinkled her nose. "I'm still not sure I trust Grant, but he didn't sell us out on the Seaside setup, so… frankly, I'm still on the fence."

"Which is the safest place to be at the moment," Mrs. Renault said, taking a seat at the table. "So, does the detective have people checking hotels and rentals for Jeff and Tamela Baker?"

"Yes, but it's going to take some time," Madison said. "There's one we've been able to eliminate."

"The one where Cray was attacked," Paul offered.

"Yes." Madison looked at Mrs. Renault. "Is there any one place that would connect to Della?"

"Several." She scanned her notebook. "Seascape on Highway 98. They stayed there in a house-hunting trip when she was assigned to the base here. Ramada resort on the island—family vacation a year earlier. Several overnight stays at Holiday Inn, usually for their New Year's Eve celebrations. And out at Delta Pointe with Jeff's parents, his sister and her family. He left a comment on the survey that he didn't want to leave."

"Maybe he came back," Madison said. "Get that information to Cray, please. And run a courtesy check on rentals in Delta Pointe."

Mrs. Renault nodded. "Jimmy, your assistance, please."

They left the conference room together.

Madison faced Paul. "There's one other thing to report. When Beech swept Vet Net the second time, he also swept here. He found a listening device planted in my office."

"Grant?" Paul asked.

"At first, I thought so." Her face burned red. "But we ran the clock, and during the window of opportunity the night our tires were slashed, he was down in the alley. Beech suspects someone helping with the flat tires the night of the festival planted the device."

"Surely not Jack Sampson."

"No. He was at Addie's when he took the call that we needed the tires fixed. A man there with experience helped. Jack didn't see the harm."

"Jeff's dad owned a repair shop and station," Paul said, recalling that from a conversation with Della. "He fixed flats all through high school."

Madison nodded. "We think it was him, and he was watching." She kept checking the door. "I'll feel better when you two are back at the ranch. It's still safest. We'll contact you as soon as we've located him."

Paul stayed stone-faced, but his eyes were a dead giveaway. "We should go to Delta Pointe and look around. It wouldn't take long." The area wasn't that big. A couple hundred properties.

"Don't you dare. He catches a glimpse of you there and he'll run so far, so fast we won't have any idea where he is."

Madison made perfect sense. "Okay. Then it's back to the ranch, provided she agrees."

"Don't worry. She will. Like Mrs. Renault said, Della's stubborn, not—"

"Madison, she's gone." Mrs. Renault rushed into the room. "Della's gone."

"How?" She had ridden with him.

"Your SUV is gone, too."

Madison fished her keys from her pocket and tossed them to Paul. "Take the Jag."

He caught them. "I'm half tempted to put a rope on that woman."

"You find her and I'll help you." Madison stood up. "We'll notify Cray."

"She's probably gone home," Mrs. Renault said. "Offering herself as bait."

"Not yet," Paul said. "Not until she's sure we're not looking for her there." He headed out the door. "She could go to Miss Addie's. She and Gracie are still out of town." Hopefully Jeff didn't know that.

"She was crying." Mrs. Renault shouted down the stairs, "Check the beach!"

"Right." Paul pushed the back door open, sprinted to the Jag, got in, cranked the engine and sped out of the parking lot.

Jeff had gone this far; he would go further. He'd go all the way.

And that put Della in grave danger.

ELEVEN

Della drove into a Starbucks drive-through, ordered her favorite and then pulled into a strip mall's parking lot to drink it while she thought through her plan.

Paul would be worried, and she hated that. But standing in the conference room, looking at the photo of Jeff's Christmas bride, Della saw one thing was too clear—he was marrying her again. They could have been twins. And that terrified Della. He'd definitely snapped, and there was no way he'd let her live and mess up the altered reality he'd created in his mind. But why would he do that? The only reason that came to mind was that he wanted to recreate what had happened—and effect a different outcome.

The coffee burned going down her throat. Better Paul worried than got caught in the cross fire—and the same for all the people who had come forward to surround her with their protection.

A couple walked past to their car, holding hands, talking.

In her mind, a snippet of conversation between her and Paul replayed.

"Are you okay?" he'd asked.

"No. But I will be." She'd clasped his hand. "I'm sorry. I hate that you've been dragged into this."

"Della, where you are, I am. You didn't do this any more than you…"

"Killed Danny?"

He nodded.

"I know."

Paul had swiveled his gaze from the road to her. "You're different. What's happened?"

"Your ranch is a special place, Paul. I'm peaceful here. I can be still and not feel empty."

She'd told him she'd made peace with God. He hadn't said a word, but tears glittered in his eyes. And at that moment, she knew love was possible. Until that moment, she believed it was lost to her forever, but in that instant she saw the truth. Love wasn't lost, just misplaced for a time. With all its ups and downs and trials and triumphs, with all its tender and rash moments, it was back. Her heart was full of love for Paul.

A warm flood of gratitude had emanated from deep within and spread through her entire body then, and it did again now.

No way was Jeff tainting that.

So she'd stolen Paul's SUV and run.

And now—she sipped from her coffee—all she had to do was lie low a couple of hours, until dark, then return to the cottage and wait for Jeff.

That he'd come after her she had no doubt.

A man walked by carrying an infant, holding the hand of a toddler girl with pigtails and a happy jack-o'-lantern on her shirt. His hair was the same color as Jeff's when the sun hit it. A car started backing out and the father shouted, "Hey, stop! Stop!" He thrust the infant forward as far as his arms would reach. "Can't you see me here with my kids?"

Mentally, she flashed back to an argument between Jeff and their next-door neighbor. He'd been outraged at the man for parking his truck on the grass a foot over the property line. He'd been belligerent; his voice had carried through the house and had her running out into the yard to see what was wrong.

Jeff surprised her, stunned her, that day. His behavior was too far over the line. The neighbor had taken serious exception to Jeff's belligerence, and the shouting match escalated. When the neighbor came charging at Jeff, he'd jerked her nearly off her feet, thrust her between them as the man just did with his baby.

He'd used her as a shield.

A shield.

Why was that significant? It was; she sensed it. But why? Having no idea, she tried to forget it, but the nagging memory wouldn't go away.

A half hour later, the memory still wouldn't fade. She dialed Detective Cray. At least taking risks was part of his job.

"Detective Cray."

"Hi, it's Della Jackson."

"Where are you?"

"Paul's already called, huh?"

"Madison. You're making our job harder."

"I'll make it easy. Don't look for me. Instead, do me a favor and I'll come in to you."

"What favor?"

"Can you get Danny's file?"

"Your son, Danny?"

"Yes." Her throat cinched.

"Della, it was a bomb. I don't think you want to burn those kinds of images into your mind."

"I don't want to, but I have to. Something is bothering me, and I—I can't explain it. I just need to see the forensic photographs in the file."

"But, Della—"

"Would you trust me?"

"All right—but it's under protest," Cray conceded. "If you'd tell me what you're looking for, I'll review them."

"I can't. I'm not sure exactly. It's a gut feeling." He was a cop. He understood a cop's gut. Computer experts and private investigators had it, too. There was a reason this memory wouldn't relent. And she didn't need to be hit with a ball bat to heed it.

"Okay, I'll make the request."

"When will you have it?"

"Depends on Tennessee. Could be a couple hours, could be a day or two. I'll ask them to rush it."

"Okay, thanks."

"This is about Jeff, not Danny, right?"

"Yeah."

"Are you still doubting he could be your stalker?"

"No, I can't say I am. But I'm not ready to convict him without indisputable evidence. Something's off. He divorced me because he blamed me for Danny. So why is he marrying a woman who looks a lot like me?"

"Tell me this request isn't linked to your emotions, Della. Tell me it's about the case."

"It's definitely about the case," she assured him, thumbing the lid on her coffee cup. Steam rose out of it and curled toward the roof of the car.

"So, where are you?"

"Starbucks, but I'm leaving." He was testing her. He'd already traced her call and knew exactly where she was.

"Della, you know he's going to come for you."

"Yes." She cranked the engine. "I'll call back to see if you've got the file."

"Wait. Della, wait."

She ended the call and removed the battery, then took off. All she had to do was stay lost awhile and then show up.

Jeff knew exactly where he'd find her.

He lay flat on his stomach under the cover of the fat bushes at the empty cottage across the street. It had been dark for hours. If she was coming back here, she should be here by now. Probably drove to Destin to avoid the crew at Lost, Inc.

They'd checked her cottage a couple of times, and she'd expect that they would.

According to his reconnaissance, everyone except Paul Mason was at Miss Addie's North Bay Café, debating where to look next to find Della.

They'd be watching the cottage—he looked at the one belonging to the old lady and the kid. No signs of life there and there hadn't been since he'd taken out Della's garage. The camera he'd installed aiming at her front door and garage proved there'd been no activity on the premises.

Della wouldn't run. That much he'd bank on. Sometime before dawn, she'd show up for the confrontation she knew now was inevitable. And where she went, Mason would follow.

Let them come. Especially Mason.

Envy, white-hot and emerald-green, ran through his veins like blood riding an adrenaline tsunami. Interfering jerk had no right to bring her here or to insinuate himself into her life.

Before dawn, he'd regret it.

They'd see that their attempts to stop him were futile and weak. They couldn't stop him. He was ready. He'd been preparing the cottage for two days....

Mason arrived in Madison McKay's Jag and parked in a driveway down the street. He checked Della's cottage, peeking in the windows. Backed away, then walked next door to Miss Addie's. In short order, he got back in the Jag and took off.

All activity stopped, and night settled in on the quiet street. No sense being in a hurry. The wee hours before dawn always made for the best disasters. When fatigue set in and weariness reigned.

Just after midnight, he heard a car. Della, driving Mason's SUV. She pulled into the driveway, headed up to the garage and parked the car in the backyard so it wasn't visible from the street. Making sure if her friends did a drive-by they wouldn't see it.

No one ever claimed she was stupid—least of all, him.

When she entered the house, he took himself a little nap. Ten minutes was enough to clear the mind and sharpen the senses. If anything disrupted the stillness, he'd know it.

He awakened and ran a neighborhood check. No strange cars, no strange activity. Calm and dead quiet. Even the wind had ceased and settled in. He waited, and waited, and finally checked his watch. 2:30 a.m.

Perfect. He scanned the street. A lamp upstairs in Della's cottage burned. Miss Addie's was dark.

No sign of Mason. Still elsewhere or lying low at Addie's so Della wouldn't know he was there?

Could be either, but it didn't matter. There'd be nothing he could do in time to save her.

He ran a final check on the rest of the neighborhood. No signs of anyone from Lost, Inc., or anyone on the street. The lights inside the homes had gone out, one by one. Everyone was down for the night. *All systems go....*

Removing the last of the surveillance cameras he'd had trained on Addie's and Della's, he stowed them in a black utility bag, retrieved the phone from his pocket and dialed the number. The telltale beep sounded. He punched in the code.

Outward, there were no signs anything had changed.

He waited three minutes, then five.

Seven minutes later, he saw the first flame through the window inside Della's.

"Goodbye, Della Jackson," he whispered, walking out of the neighborhood. "Have a pleasant death."

Something was burning.

Fully dressed on her bed, unaware that she'd drifted off to sleep, Della startled awake. Her hand clipped her cell phone. It crashed against the floor and cracked. Her nose burned. Fire. Definitely fire. She ran to her bedroom door. It was hot, and smoke began pouring into her bedroom under her door.

Second floor. Only way out was the window. She turned for it. Unlocked its latches and heaved.

Someone had nailed it shut.

She grabbed the house phone. *Dead.* Tried the cell, though she had no hope it was functional. It wasn't.

Think, Della. Think!

She had to get out. She swept the nightstand bare, lifted it and heaved it against the window. It bounced, but the glass didn't break.

She touched it—it wasn't glass. Her window had been replaced with some kind of acrylic. Shatterproof acrylic.

The smoke thickened, burning her eyes, her lungs. She stood on her bed, reached for the ceiling. If she could get into the attic, she might be able to bust through the eaves or even the roof. She stretched, but was too short. Couldn't reach.

Returning to the window, she banged on it and shouted. Someone would hear her. Someone somewhere had to hear her. "Help! Help!"

A loud thump sounded.

A ladder appeared against the side of the house. And then Paul's face appeared at the window. "Move away from the window."

Never in her life had she been so glad to see anyone. "I can't get out."

He motioned for her to move.

Della stepped aside, and he rammed a crowbar against the pane. Nothing happened. Quickly assessing, he dragged his fingertips along the edge and began prying out the acrylic sheet. "Jimmy, it's Plexiglas," he shouted down the ladder. "Heads up."

The outer sheet fell to the ground.

Della's eyes burned, watering so bad everything was blurred. Her throat and lungs ached. She couldn't think straight, and coughed hard, then harder. Her knees went weak, then gave out. Too weak to catch herself, she slid down to the floor.

Paul watched her sink down out of his view. "Della! Hang on, Della!"

He rammed the inner sheet with his shoulder. Again and again.

The wood beside it cracked and gave. He raised it as a shield against the flames now creeping into her bedroom, stepping over Della, on the floor.

She was unconscious.

Please... Paul gathered her in his arms and made his way down the ladder. Jimmy steadied it from the ground.

Paul ran away from the house and put Della down on the ground in the grass, forced fresh air into her lungs. He pressed his fingertips to her neck. "Get an ambulance."

"On the way," Jimmy told him. "Is she okay?"

Paul looked up, his face wet with tears from the stinging fire, from fear of losing Della. "She has a pulse."

He repeated that into his phone, then asked, "Her lungs? Are they burned?"

"I don't know. I think I got to her in time. I just don't know."

He kept breathing for her. "Della, please don't leave me, too. Please, don't you leave me, too."

Della sputtered and coughed.

Her eyes burned, stung. "Paul?"

"Right here, honey." He clasped her hand. "You're okay. You're in an ambulance. There was a fire."

"I remember. The windows..." Her voice was thick and raspy, and her throat felt raw. "I can't see. Everything is blurry."

"There's salve in your eyes to protect them. You'll be okay."

"I couldn't get out."

He pressed his face to their clasped hands. "You're out now. Everything is going to be fine."

"Fine?" Worry rippled through her voice.

"Not fine," he quickly amended. "Great. It's all going to be great." He shouted at the driver, "How much longer?"

"Two minutes."

Della went statue still. She'd know that voice anywhere. Oh, no. *No.*

"I'm going to give you a shot to help with the pain, Miss Jackson." A female attendant wearing an awful blond wig that half hid her face filled a syringe.

"No. I don't want it."

"It'll help your body heal, not to have to fight the pain."

"No." Della felt the IV in her arm. "Take it out, Paul. I want it out. Right now."

"Della, you need fluids." He seemed totally oblivious. "Let me talk to her," he told the female attendant. "She's disoriented."

"Just for a minute. She's going to need this when we move her."

Paul leaned low, whispered, "What's wrong?"

She drew on his hand. *J. E. F. F.*

"You want Jeff?"

She pressed a fingertip to her lips, mouthed, *Jeff is driving.*

Paul nodded, adjusted the IV, removed the needle and repaired the dressing, burying it so it appeared that the needle was still inserted in her vein.

"Okay," the female EMT said. "We really can't wait any longer."

Finally he'd gotten a good look at the EMT. It was the woman who'd posed as Della and shipped the package from Panama City. "No problem," Paul said, thinking on his feet. "She's ready now, right?"

"It doesn't hurt, but okay."

Tamela injected something into the IV line, emptied the syringe.

Della reached for Paul. "Don't leave me."

"I won't." He stroked her arm. "Trust me."

The ambulance stopped at a traffic light. Its red lights whipped circles into the darkness and its siren blared. The driver honked at the cars ahead, signaling them to get out of his way.

Paul seized his preoccupation, elbowed the attendant—Tamela in a wig—knocked her out, then positioned her so that the top half of her body was hidden from the driver's view, and it appeared that she was bent over Della.

Ready? he mouthed.

Della nodded.

He grabbed her, shoved open the back door and jumped through, tugged her into his arms, then took off running with her down the street.

Madison honked. "Get in. Get in!"

Paul dumped Della into the backseat, then slid into the passenger's seat, banging his knee on the dash. Pain shot up his leg. "Go. Go!"

Madison stomped the accelerator, made a U-turn and sped down the street. "Cray, hold on," she said into her phone. "I don't know what's going on. Paul will explain." Madison thrust the phone at him.

Paul seated it at his ear. "Jeff Jackson's driving the ambulance. Tamela Baker's playing the EMT. Della recognized his voice. Tamela tried to give her a shot of something, so check the syringe." He quickly explained the rest. He turned to look at Della. "Don't touch the bandages. Cray wants to analyze them."

"Okay."

"You all right, Della?" Madison spoke softly.

"Yeah, I am. I think I really am."

"Thank God," Paul said. "Finally some good news. Let me know when you have him. Yeah, call Madison's cell." Paul disconnected, told Della and Madison, "They've intercepted the ambulance. Tamela's in custody. She says Jeff took off on foot when we escaped. Officers haven't spotted him yet, but if he's on foot, it shouldn't be long until they have him in custody."

Tears slid down Della's cheeks. "They have to find him first."

"They will." Paul looked beyond her, checking behind them.

"Doc has a hotel room he wants us to see." Madison looked back at Della in the rearview. "Do you need the hospital?"

"No, no hospital. The oxygen was real and my eyes are clearing." She shoved her hair back from her face. "What happened to the real EMTs?" Chills ripped up Della's back. "You don't think he's hurt—"

"Cray doesn't think anyone was involved. Tamela says Jeff stole the empty ambulance from the drive at the hospital and was waiting to rush in—if Della made it out, that is. Cray's verifying things now."

Della squeezed her eyes shut, hoping no one was hurt.

"You're sure you're okay? What about your breathing?" Paul asked. "Any burning or pain when you breathe deep?"

He was worried about her lungs. "A little heavy, but no scorched taste in my mouth, and none of the other indications. A little scratchy throat, but it's already feeling better. I'm okay."

"Good." Madison passed back an evidence bag. "Put that IV dressing in this."

Paul gently removed the IV dressing and dropped it all into the bag, sealed it then passed it back to Madison.

Madison caught Della's gaze in the rearview. "Are you up to seeing whatever it is Doc wants us to see?"

Paul checked the side mirrors, then scanned the street out the back windshield, making sure they weren't being followed. Diligent. What a blessing he'd been nearby. She'd needed him many times in the past three years, but never more than tonight. "Yeah, I'm up to it." Adrenaline still surged through her body. The sooner this was resolved, the better. "Where's this hotel?"

"Delta Pointe," Madison said. "We found the one Jeff stayed in with his family—the one he didn't want to leave. Apparently a couple homes were taken out in Hurricane Opal. The land sat vacant for a couple years, and then a developer bought it, razed it and built a hotel where it used to be. Doc's there now."

It was undoubtedly close enough to possibly be Jeff-related. Her stomach pitched. "Has he called Cray?"

Madison tilted her head. "Actually, Cray contacted Doc after hotel management called the police."

"Why did the hotel call the police?" Paul asked.

Della braced for the worst.

"I don't know." Madison smoothed a hand down her slim black skirt. "Doc didn't want to discuss it over the phone."

Della looked at Paul. The concern in Madison's voice didn't begin to convey the worry so evident in his eyes.

TWELVE

Madison parked at Delta Pointe.

The sky-blue clapboard hotel stretched four stories high and for all intents appeared to be a large home with a half dozen white wicker rockers on a front porch that stretched all the way across its width. "It's room 205," she told Della, glancing through the car window at her.

Paul climbed out, his cell phone at his ear, and then opened the door for Della. "Okay," he said into the phone. "No, it's not good news. Let us know if you spot him."

Della stepped out of Madison's car. The salty tang of gulf breeze blew in her face and filled her senses, but the calm that usually came with it eluded her. "Was that Cray calling?" Fear burned in her stomach.

"Yeah, he'll be here shortly. He was detained."

"Bad news obviously." It didn't take a rocket scientist to decipher Paul's tone or expression. Add what she'd overheard of their conversation, and the truth was evident. "Jeff got away, didn't he?"

The stiff breeze tugged at his hair. Paul bit down on his lips. "For now."

She wanted to cry. Her nose burned and her eyes stung.

"Cray's got every available officer on it and he's issued an APB. Okaloosa and Walton counties are on alert."

She nodded, too well aware there were a million ways to

slip through the net, especially by cutting through all the reservation land. He'd been on a four-wheeler at the ranch, so he had the means to do it. Definitely not good news. "Can't anything break our way? Just one thing?"

"A lot has." Madison gripped her hair in a bunch at her neck to keep it from flying in her face.

"Like what?"

"Well, you're not dead. Neither explosion got you, and the attempted ones failed to go off. And you escaped from the fire. That's a lot of big breaks right there." Madison sighed. "Look, don't get discouraged, Della. You know how these things go. He'll mess up and we'll get him. They always mess up, and you always get them."

She did. She had. That's the highest form of praise Madison McKay had ever given her. Total, unconditional faith in her competence.

"What?" Madison asked, perplexed.

"Nothing," Della whispered.

Clearly oblivious that her words meant so much, Madison started walking toward the building. "Room's on the second floor."

Paul clasped her shoulder. "She's right, you know. A lot has broken our way and you will get him."

"I know. I just want things to get—"

"Easier?"

She looked up at Paul. "Yes. Exactly. It's been a hard three years and I'm weary. I need a little bliss. Actually, I wouldn't mind more than a little bliss."

"You'll get it. That's a promise. This, too, shall pass."

Madison looked back at Della. "If I had to face half of what you've dealt with, I don't know if I'd still be upright. You're my hero." Madison took a sip of her sweet tea. A bit dribbled and she quickly swiped it up. For some reason she was in Mrs. Renault's car and it was as impeccable as the woman who owned it. "When I grow up, I want half your strength."

Stunned, Della smiled. She had no idea Madison felt that way. "You already have more."

"No, actually, I don't. I'm learning, watching you."

Della didn't know what to say to that. She wouldn't have thought it for a second. Madison was always quick, decisive and steadfast. She always seemed to have it together and to know exactly what to do, acting with confidence, and she was certainly self-reliant and assured. These comments seemed so out of character for her, but in a way, were they really? How many times had she said, "Fake it till you make it"? Madison was faking confidence and strength—well, kind of, anyway. She was acting on leaps of faith, trusting that strength would come. Acting as if she already had it, trusting she'd get what she needed.

There was a lesson in that.

There was—probably several of them.

They entered the wide front door. A compass had been in-laid in teak in the center of the lobby floor. Straight ahead was a check-in desk. To the right was a wide spiral staircase and to the right of it a wooden elevator. Taking the stairs, they headed up to the second floor and then walked down the soft gray hall-way to room 205. "Here it is," she said, a little surprised. From the hallway, it seemed nothing was amiss.

Madison knocked on the door. "Ian?"

"It's okay." Though muffled, Doc's voice carried into the hall. "It's Madison McKay." The door opened.

"Della. Paul." Doc motioned them inside. "Sorry about the cottage." He studied her. "You okay?"

"I'm fine." Seeing Paul's head jerk in her direction, she re-called his aversion to the word. "I'm okay, really," she amended.

Four officers stood in the room. All were stoic, intense and busy. One took photographs, another dusted surfaces of tables, lamps, the remote for the television. The other two stood star-ing into a closet, jotting notes on two separate pads. Della got a weird, sick feeling. Nothing seemed odd in the room itself.

Whatever Doc had called them here to see was clearly inside the closet that had captured all their interest.

Paul stepped forward. "What did you find?"

"Is Della really okay?" Doc asked in a stage whisper. "I mean, can she take a shock?"

"She can hear you, and she can take a shock." She answered for herself. "She's absorbed a mountain of them, and she's still aboveground and upright."

Madison nodded.

"The housekeeper found this and reported it to the manager. He took one look and called the police."

Della followed Doc's hand signal and looked into the closet. Taped to the back wall were a dozen photographs of her and her son. Her at her wedding…at the hospital, holding Danny for the first time…playing with him on the floor before the Christmas tree…and they were all mutilated. Neither she nor Danny had eyes!

"These are of you and Danny, right?" Doc asked. "They seem to be, but Tamela Baker looks a lot like you. We couldn't be sure."

"They're Danny and me." Tears trickled down her cheeks.

If each photo hadn't evoked a specific memory in her mind, even she wouldn't be able to say without a doubt. All the faces were slashed. She stared at them in horror until she couldn't bear to look at them anymore. Rage flared in her belly, burned as hot as the fire at the cottage. She'd begged, begged, for three solid years for one photo. Just one, and he'd done this? A keening sound escaped from her throat.

She looked away, determined to squelch it. And on the floor of the closet below them sat something that raised the threat again with a vengeance.

A pair of neon-blue aquatic shoes.

Della and Paul dropped Madison off at her home on the bay, switched from Mrs. Renault's sedan to Madison's Jag and then took it to the ranch, where their protective detail should be waiting.

Paul hadn't pushed Della to talk on the long ride home. She was grateful for that. Seeing those photos of Danny and her slashed...it was just the last straw. She'd hit her limit on endurable body slams. If one more thing happened, she was apt to pop her cork, as Miss Addie liked to say, or more likely, collapse into the fetal position and just stay that way.

When they arrived at the ranch, Jake met them just inside the gate.

At the head of the driveway near the ranch house, Warny stood waiting, shotgun in hand. She braced herself for gunfire and falling tree limbs—they were in a strange vehicle—but he didn't shoot. Did he recognize Madison's car?

Paul stopped the Jag and they got out.

"Out of ammo?" Della attempted a little levity.

His face seemed carved of stone and lined with worry. "Madison called and warned me you were in her car. The detail's been detained but should be here shortly. Bad wreck on the interstate."

"Ah." Madison knew of his tree-shooting penchant. Not surprised. Word traveled fast in a small community like North Bay.

"Jack Sampson told me about the fire. He says you were unconscious and you had to escape from the ambulance on the way to the hospital. You okay, Miss Della?"

"Fit as a fiddle, thank you."

"Jack kind of feels responsible since he hired the tire-slasher. Wants you to know he's real sorry about that and he and his family are hunting down that Jeff Jackson. He says Jeff's the same guy."

She had to smile. "It's not Jack's fault, Warny. When you talk to him, tell him. The man fooled me, too, and I was..." She couldn't make herself say it. "I should have known better." If she'd listened to her instincts, she would have. But she'd been so hesitant to blame him because she'd been falsely blamed. Sometimes it was hard to find the line between being fair and foolish.

Paul petted Jake. "Everything okay here?"

"Right as rain. Jake and me's been patrolling since Jack called. We ain't seen a thing."

"Good news." Paul seemed as eager for it as Della felt. "Thanks, Warny."

"She's swaying on her feet, son." Warny motioned to Della. "Best get her settled in afore she drops like a stone." He looked down to the alert rottweiler. "Jake, you watch her, boy."

He barked.

A half hour later, Della was bathed and shampooed and free of the stink of smoke and the fire. She dried off and changed into a clean T-shirt and pajama pants and then lay snug in bed in the buttery-yellow room.

Exhausted from the heart out, she closed her eyes, expressed her silent gratitude for her life. For Paul sensing something was wrong, for getting her out of that burning house. And for helping her recognize Jeff's voice and not blurt out anything that got anyone hurt. She was grateful for much more…for having Madison follow them in Mrs. Renault's car and get them away from Jeff. And for giving Paul the foresight to get that IV needle out of her arm. She was grateful…for everything.

Images of those horribly disfigured photos filled her mind and haunted her. "Go away," she whispered. Maybe Cray would catch Jeff and she could remember something not terrible. "It doesn't have to be something good, just something not terrible."

A vision of Danny and her on the beach building a sand castle formed in her mind. She grabbed it and held on, wishing Paul could see it, too, and then lost herself in the joyful memory of that day.

The next morning at breakfast, Cray called and Paul talked with him, then rejoined Della and Warny at the kitchen table.

The smell of sausage omelets and homemade biscuits still filled the air.

Warny buttered his third, then smeared on strawberry jam. "I like your cooking, Miss Della."

She smiled. "It's fun to have someone to cook for again."

"I still can't believe you like it, but I think I'll get used to it fast." Paul grinned, but as he returned to the table, his smile faded. "They haven't found Jeff," he told her. "The file photos from Tennessee came in. Cray's having an officer drive them out."

She nodded. Sipped her coffee.

"Della, I wish you wouldn't look at them. Let me. You don't need to see—"

"I do."

"Why?"

"I don't know, but I need to see them."

Warny took his dishes to the sink, limping badly. "What's wrong with your leg?" She hadn't noticed him limp last night, but he hadn't really moved much, either.

"Knee's out again," he said. "Thunder stumbled yesterday and banged me against a tree. I woke up near lame this morning."

"Do you need to see the doctor? I can call—"

"Naw, the vet was out checking the horses, so he took a look. Said to stay off it and ice it down. No riding today."

"Go sit in the recliner and kick your feet up," Paul said. "I'll bring you an ice pack."

"I got my own recliner, but I'll take the ice pack. I'm reading me a book I want to get back to in the barn."

"I can get your book."

"I want my chair—in my barn, son."

"Let me fix you an ice pack, then." Della pulled out a ziplock bag and filled it with a mixture of crushed and cubed ice, then rifled through the freezer and found a bag of frozen peas.

"These work better." She passed the peas and then the ice pack. "They conform to the shape of your leg."

He looked skeptical.

"Miss Addie uses them all the time."

"All righty, then. Thanks." Warny took them both and then headed to the back door, pausing to scan the monitors.

"Everything look okay?" Paul asked.

"Yep."

"I'll exercise the horses till your knee gets better." The air smelled of rain.

He nodded. "Best get to it, then. Thunder gets stiff if he ain't walked before ten."

Paul smiled. "As soon as I help Della with the kitchen."

Warny left, and Jake got his bites from them both. "You go on," she said. "I can get this."

"You sure?"

She nodded. "If Warny thinks you're cutting it too close, he'll go exercise Thunder anyway, and you know it."

"He will." Paul's expression softened. "It's best. I want to be back before the rain gets here."

"And before the photos come."

"That, too. The alarm will be off, so stay alert."

"I will." Thoughtful, she set her dishes on the counter and tiptoed to kiss his cheek. "You are such a blessing, Paul Mason."

"I'm blessed." He kissed her, closing his arms around her and pulling her close.

Jake barked.

Paul frowned at him. "Warny made him do that. I know he did."

Della laughed. "You're probably right about that."

"Guard." Paul grabbed his hat, checked the monitors then headed to the door. "I'll be back as soon as I can. Remember, you're alone with no protection. Stay alert."

"The detail should be here any minute. And I'm armed." She smiled, giving the dog a pat. "We're fine, aren't we, Jake?"

He wagged his tail.

Paul went outside and Jake went barreling after him, whining and whimpering at the back door closing, shutting him inside. Paul had been gone a lot lately and Jake hadn't gotten out and run. Now he was champing at the bit to join Paul.

Della's heart couldn't take the sad pleading in his eyes. "All right." She opened the door. "Go to him, boy."

Jake took off like a shot, his stride long, his ears slicking back.

Della watched him go. "Now, that's a happy puppy." She smiled, couldn't not smile, and it occurred to her that despite all their trials and challenges, she was happy, too. She braced for the guilt that always followed, but it didn't come.

Maybe finally she was healing. She finished cleaning the kitchen and set the cast-iron skillet she'd made biscuits in back into the oven to dry.

When she turned to put the dish towel on the counter, she gasped.

A uniformed officer stood in the kitchen, holding a brown manila envelope. His hat shadowed his eyes and concealed too much of his face. "Don't you knock?"

"I did. No one answered," he said in a low gravelly voice. "I was afraid something was wrong, so I came to check."

He hadn't knocked. She would have heard it. "Everything's fine. Thank you." She reached out for the envelope. "This is the information from Detective Cray, correct?"

"I'm supposed to give it to Mr. Mason."

A cold chill swept up her back. Her gun was in the bedroom. She needed a weapon. "Paul?" she called out.

No answer, of course.

She feigned surprise at that. "Just a minute, let me get him." She took two steps. "Paul." She raised her voice. "The protective detail's arrived with the info from Detective—"

He spun her around by the shoulder, shoved back his hat. "He's not here and you're not getting this information, Della." The .45 in his hand was aimed at her.

"Jeff." Her heart beat harder, faster. She mentally talked herself calm. *Don't panic. He'll kill you. Don't panic.* "What do you want?"

"My son."

She hiked her chin. "Me, too."

The veins in his neck bulged. "I thought it would get better with time. It hasn't."

"No." She borrowed a line from Miss Addie, slowly scanned, looking for something to defend herself with but spotting nothing. "It doesn't get better," she told him. "We just get better at dealing with it."

"I knew you'd do this." He waved the envelope. "It was just a matter of time."

"What are you talking about?"

"Don't play stupid. That might work with Mason, but not with me. I know you."

Having no idea what to say, she stayed silent. Fear coiled inside her. He wanted her dead, but worse, he wanted her to suffer. Why? How could he not know she had suffered? She still suffered.

"It took you longer to figure it out than I thought it would. Course, you haven't seen the pictures, so I guess that's why."

"I saw the photos you left at Delta Pointe." She frowned at him. The smell of biscuits had been so good earlier. Now the scent seemed heavy and cloying. "Why did you cut our faces, Jeff? Why would you do that to Danny and me?"

"What are you talking about?"

"Don't even go there." He did think she was stupid. What did he fear she would see in the pictures? What did he fear she would figure out? What did he not want Danny or her to see? Or was it that he didn't want them to see him? She didn't have a clue.

"You won't get pictures of him." His big body shook. "Not now, not ever."

"Why not? Did you destroy all of them? Blind our son in all of them, Jeff? Why did you do that? What are you trying to stop Danny and me from seeing?"

His eyes widened.

"That's it. You blinded us so that we couldn't see it. The man you really are. That's what you were doing. That's why you're terrified of me seeing the photographs in that envelope. You're terrified enough to kill me to keep your secret. But what makes you think the truth is still a secret, Jeff?" She frowned at him and faked knowing what he obviously thought she knew. She changed tactics to confuse him. "What I still don't get is Tamela. Why get involved with a woman who has to remind you of me? You hate me, so why would you do that? Had to be because you needed her to ship the package, which makes me wonder why she would agree. Did you threaten her, too, Jeff?"

"I'm marrying her."

"See? Now, that's just odd. Why are you marrying me all over again? It doesn't make sense."

"She's nothing like you. With you, the military came first. I got what was left. Danny, too."

How dare he! How dare he! "I was a good wife and a good mother. Don't you dare say I wasn't."

"You were never there. If you'd been there—"

"I'd be dead and Danny would be alive," she finished for him. "Do you think I haven't wished that a thousand times? Do you think I don't know it?" She paused, calmed the shrill from her voice. "But this isn't about that. Not really. Tamela certainly isn't—"

"You forget what this is about. Just forget it. It doesn't matter anymore."

"If it doesn't matter, then why are you trying to kill me over it?"

"If I wanted you dead, you'd be dead."

"Jeff, let's be real. You've put considerable effort into killing me. You've just failed."

"That's not true." He raised the gun and took a two-handed aim.

No fear. The minute he thought he'd won, he'd pull the trigger. "Oh, really?" She crossed her arms over her chest to hide her shaking. "What was in that syringe? Arsenic? Cyanide? Tamela was determined to give it to me."

"She did give it to you. I watched her."

"And that perplexes you—that it didn't kill me."

"Just shut up." He waved the gun at her, agitated, his face sunburn red. "She's in jail and I want her out."

Della guffawed. "The two of you tried to kill me and you think I'm going to help you?"

The back door opened without a sound and Jake and Paul entered, their movements stealth, silent.

"Your choice," Jeff said, his tone threatening. "You can help me or die."

Jake lunged and latched on to Jeff's arm.

Paul knocked the gun from his hand, kicked it across the floor to Della.

Jeff swung at Paul. Jake dangled off the floor, his teeth sunk into Jeff's forearm.

Della grabbed the gun. Cocked it and shouted. "Stop!" She spread her legs, took a two-handed aim at Jeff's chest. "Don't make me kill you. I don't want to do it, but I will."

Jeff looked at her as if she'd lost her mind. "You're not going to kill me."

"Yes, Jeff." She gave him a flat, steady look. "I will."

Something flashed in his eyes and then crossed his face. He believed her and stilled.

"Jake, heel."

He let go, backed off and sat down within lunging distance. Alert, ready.

Paul took the envelope. Praised Jake. Then called Detective

Cray. "I've got Jeff Jackson in my kitchen. He pulled a gun on Della. Now she's got it trained on him and if he moves, she's going to shoot him, so don't linger getting here." A brief pause, then, "No, she's not hysterical. She's a marksman, combat veteran." Another quick pause. "No, I am not going to take the gun away from her. He's tried to kill her several times. If she has to shoot him, she will shoot him. Home invasion, self-defense."

Paul was playing to Jeff's fears. Della kept the gun trained on him. They both knew she wouldn't shoot him unless provoked.

Paul hung up, stowed his phone and stepped too close to Jeff.

Seizing the opportunity, Jeff whipped his good arm back and hit Paul upside the head.

"Jake, stay!" Della shouted. "Jeff, move again, and you're a dead man—I mean it."

"You'd never bloody a clean floor."

"You have no idea what I will or won't do. The woman you knew is gone. I'm not her anymore. I warn you, don't try me, Jefferson Jackson. You won't survive to regret it." She motioned with her chin. "Paul, get some rope."

"What about first aid for his arm? He's bleeding pretty bad."

"Let him bleed." It wasn't that bad. Jake could have taken his arm off, but he hadn't. Nothing Jeff couldn't stand. Glaring at him, she added, "Blowing up my garage. Burning down my cottage. I should shoot you just for general principles."

Jeff frowned. "Woman, have you lost your mind?"

"Now's not a good time to push her." Paul returned with the rope, shoved Jeff onto a chair, then began tying him up.

"She was my wife." His eyes sparked hostility. "Don't you tell me—"

"Fine." Paul lifted his hand. "But she's not that woman anymore."

Ignoring him, Jeff spat at Della. "I had nothing to do with your garage or your cottage. You're crazy if you think you're pinning that on me."

Paul took the envelope and passed it to Della.

She exchanged it for the gun. Paul looked at Jeff. "Don't even think about moving."

Jeff's face bleached white.

Della opened the envelope. Fourteen photographs spilled into her hands. Each of them shattered her heart. Her eyes blurred. She swiped at them and made herself keep looking. God, give her strength. Carry her.

On the eleventh photo she saw what Jeff feared she'd see. "Paul."

He stepped to her side. "Look at the splatter."

Her heart, though seized and crushed, somehow held the pain.

"Don't show it to him. Don't!" Jeff screamed, and tears streaked down his face.

"I'm so sorry." Paul clasped her shoulder. "I—I don't know what to say."

She walked over to Jeff and slapped his face. Then slapped him again.

Jake didn't move. Didn't growl or utter a sound, just watched her carefully as if sensing her sadness and shock. She raised her hand to slap Jeff a third time.

"Della, enough," Paul said from behind her.

She stopped midswing. What was she thinking? Doing? *No. No, I won't be like him. I won't.* The anger churning inside her threatened to erupt yet again and smother out everything good. So strong and fierce and unrelenting it frightened her. She stiffened, shunned it, prayed for calm and a clear mind.

Paul stepped closer, lowered her arm and closed his arms around her. "It's okay. Everything's going to be okay."

She buried her face in his shoulder and cried deep, heavy sobs wrenched from her soul. Her entire body shook, racked by spasms. Jake moved closer, nuzzled her leg with his nose. "He knew," she told Paul, then glared at Jeff. "You saw the wires. You couldn't have missed seeing the wires. And you opened the box anyway." She curled the fabric of Paul's shirt into her fist to keep from lashing out again. "You knew and you used our baby as a shield to protect yourself. How could you do that? How could you…do that?"

Jeff stared down at his lap and said nothing.

"You knew I would know it because you did it to me—our neighbor who parked on the grass and you went postal. But that's one thing, Jeff. Danny? A baby? Our baby?" A scream tortured her throat. She tried to break away from Paul, to go after Jeff again.

Paul held her tight. "No. No."

Giving up, she let out a deep, keening scream that held three years of self-recrimination and guilt and grief and agony. Three years of regret and blame and self-loathing for not being there to protect her child when he needed protection. And shame and disgust that what he'd needed protection from most was his own father.

Warny hobbled into the kitchen with his shotgun. "What in tarnation is going on—?" He stopped, looked at Della, saw her pain and asked Paul, "That him?"

Paul nodded.

"Get her where she don't have to look at him."

"No." She sniffed. "No." She walked over and jerked back Jeff's head, forced him to look into her eyes. "You look at me, Jefferson Jackson." She waited until he opened his eyes and his gaze met hers. "You were ashamed of yourself. Terrified I'd know the truth—that anyone would discover it. You hid like a coward behind our baby and that's why you blamed me. That's why you divorced me. Not because it was my fault. Because it was yours, and you were scared to death I'd know it. So scared you were willing to kill me to keep the truth hidden. So no one else would see what you've done. Well, I'm alive, and I see. I'm not blind and I know. I'll always know."

"I thought it was a joke."

"A joke?" She grunted. "With some of your friends, maybe.

But you still put Danny between you and the box, so somewhere in your head, you thought it might not be a joke. All you had to do was back off and call the cops. That's all."

"I didn't want to look stupid if it was a joke."

"Well, congratulations. You don't look stupid. You look just like the coward you were, hiding behind an innocent child."

He withered on the chair and closed his eyes.

She let go of his head. "Detective Cray's here. I hear the car." She told Paul and then looked back at Jeff. "You know what, Jeff? You're going to have to live with yourself for the things you've done to Danny and to me. A long time of it, you'll live in jail. But I want you to know something. Once you leave here today, I'll mourn my son. And then I'm going to live my life. It'll be rich and full and I'll be content and happy." The fire left her voice. "And on the rare occasion when you cross my mind, I'll pray for you. One day, I might even be able to forgive you. But it won't be today."

She turned and walked out of the kitchen.

He sat alone at the farthermost white-resin table in the sea of white-resin tables and chairs. Metal framing stretched up and overhead, forming a green tent-type tarpaulin ceiling. That and a tiled concrete slab formed the outdoor dining room of Miss Addie's North Bay Café.

A fan stirred the air. Near the blue front wall that led into the indoor dining room and kitchen sat all of the Lost, Inc., staff. Laughing and talking over dessert, they were having a fine time. Della Jackson sat between Grant Deaver and Paul Mason.

He hadn't killed her, though he'd tried often enough—too often to try again and reveal that everything hadn't been sewn up nice and tidy in a perfect little package. At least he'd gotten to see her fear.

Some sacrifices were worth making for the benefit gained in having Jeff Jackson blamed for everything.

Pulling out his wallet, he dropped a tip on the table and

then exited off the slab and cut across the lawn to the sidewalk. Under the shade of an encroaching oak, he lit a cigar. Jackson didn't know one end of a triggering device from another, but no one believed him. He'd be convicted for it all and do a nice long stint in jail.

If he hadn't done what he'd done to his kid, his whole future would have been different. But he did. And because he did, no one would be looking for the man who really had done everything except ship a package and steal an ambulance. Jeff Jackson would be blamed for it all.

Two women came toward him on the sidewalk. Nodding, he stepped aside so they could pass. "Ladies."

They smiled.

He walked on. Unfortunately, he still needed someone to blame for the security breach at the Nest. The human blood on the knives came back with no matches, just as he intended, so they were stymied on that aspect of the investigation. Jackson was convenient, but without access through Della, no one would consider him a viable suspect for the Nest security breach. He glanced over at the Lost, Inc., staff, seated now just off his left shoulder. No, for that crime he needed someone with access, motive, means and opportunity. He needed one of them.

He'd like to set up that rich snob Madison McKay, but Deaver was too close to her at the moment, so he didn't dare. That left Jimmy, Mrs. Renault and Ian Crane, aka Doc. Which one would it be?

He paused at the bench and studied them. He'd decide soon.

Della wasn't dead and had been absolved for the security breach of the Nest. That was a disappointment, but as he'd aptly proven, there are times when it's harder to live with the truth than it is to die.

She'd discovered that, and it was clear now that the cowardly Jeff Jackson had, too.

He pulled three coins from his pocket: a quarter, a dime and a nickel—Doc, Mrs. Renault and Jimmy. *Heads or tails. Odd one out becomes the Nest's next victim.*

He flipped the coins.

EPILOGUE

Della and Paul joined the Lost, Inc., group in the conference room.

Madison hugged her hard. "He's in jail. I'm so glad this is behind you."

A flurry of comments came from the others.

"You sleeping okay, Della?" Doc asked.

"I am now." She nodded at Mrs. Renault, sitting with her pen poised over her pad.

"We've been calling Warny. He says you're okay."

Paul pulled out her chair. She sat down. "I am. I just needed a few days to come to grips with everything."

"Of course you did." Mrs. Renault reached over and patted her arm. "Miss Addie is back home. She's overseeing the workers at the cottage."

"They've started repairs?"

Mrs. Renault nodded. "Sampson Construction. They've promised Miss Addie they'll have everything done in a month."

"That's good news." She glanced at Paul.

His reaction seemed mixed. "Stay at the ranch as long as you like. It's good for you there."

"It is. Thank you. But what about Warny's snoring?"

"Warny snores?" Paul didn't smile, but his eyes twinkled. "I hadn't noticed."

She laughed, then swiped her hair back from her face. "I can't begin to thank you all for everything you've done to help me through this. There just…aren't words."

Madison smiled. "Della, we're family, and wouldn't have it any other way. I wish we could have spared you from some of the…bad parts of this, but now you know the truth, and he won't be able to hurt you anymore."

"No, he won't." She still had a hard time wrapping her mind around Jeff's actions.

Jimmy slumped sideward, chewing a wad of gum. "Is he still denying everything?"

"Aside from the ambulance snatch," Paul said. "Tommy and his dad went down for a lineup, but Tommy says Jeff isn't the man who approached him on the sidewalk. Cray figures he hired someone, maybe a tourist."

"Does he have enough to convict him?" Grant Deaver asked.

"He says he does," Della said, thoroughly weary of being the topic of the conversation. "So, what about the security breach at the Nest?"

Madison shot a worried look at Grant.

"Not that it'll come as a surprise to anyone, but I was hauled in and disclosed the attempt to sting at Seaside—not to randomly report or disclose but to substantiate my assertion that there was nothing at Lost, Inc., or with any of you to support any claim that the Nest breach started here with one or more of you."

Madison stilled. "You defended us to them?"

He nodded. "I couldn't ignore their summons. Everyone here knows you're subject to recall after you depart the fix and separate from active duty. I couldn't lie, so I told the truth in a way that was honest and, I believe, accurate."

Madison covered his hand with hers. "Thank you for telling us, Grant."

Della watched Madison's expression change, mercurial.

Definitely attracted, definitely troubled by the attraction and clearly seeking reassurance. She swerved her gaze to Grant and saw the same uncertainty in him.

"Love and distrust is a real pain in a relationship," Paul whispered.

"It is," she whispered back, wondering which would win between them.

"So, where does that leave us?" Jimmy cracked his gum, earning himself a strong visual reprimand from Mrs. Renault. "Mmm, sorry."

Grant took in a sharp breath. "Right now they're looking elsewhere."

"Which means we're neither on nor off the hook." Madison accepted it.

"In these situations that's the best it gets, Madison." Mrs. Renault smiled. "This is good news. If they had anything at all, we'd be arrested. So we're in good shape."

Doc's stomach growled. "Did you say Miss Addie's back?" he asked Mrs. Renault.

"I did."

"Is she cooking today?"

Mrs. Renault nodded. "Yes, she is."

"Well, if we're done here, I'm going to see if she's made any banana pudding."

"That sounds good. I love her banana pudding." Jimmy stood up. "Let's go."

Mrs. Renault closed her pad. "I could use some strawberry shortcake."

"Ooh, me, too." Madison stood up.

Grant followed her. "Pecan pie."

"Ooh, I want a bite. Miss Addie makes the best pecan pie." Madison grabbed her handbag, looked at Paul and Della. "You guys coming?"

"No," Paul said. "Della made a peach cobbler."

"You cooked?" Madison looked flabbergasted.

Della laughed. "I'm a great cook."

Madison patted her chest. "Keep beating, heart. Keep beating." She moved to the door. "Take a week off, Della. Just be for a little while. Ian's up to speed on all your cases and you need some downtime. You haven't taken a day off in three years."

Della nodded. "Thanks. I'm going to take you up on that. Warny's planting a garden. I could help him with it. His eyes aren't so good right now."

"They'd be fine if he'd wear his glasses," Paul said. "But he'd love your help."

"Mmm." Madison smiled. "Good. This is good."

"Yes." Della smiled back, and Madison left, calling down the stairs, "Wait for me."

Grant's voice carried back. "I'm waiting. Seems I spend half my life waiting for you."

Della looked at Paul. "Think they'll make it?"

He debated. "Wrong question."

"What's the right question?"

"Will they be sane when they make it, or drive each other crazy in the process?"

Della laughed, snagged his arm and squeezed.

"You okay? Really?"

"I will be." She looked up, let him see all there was to see in her eyes. "I'm so much better."

Relief washed down Paul's face. "It's been hard on you, I know."

"On you, too, but that wasn't what I meant. It's not what I got rid of. It's what I found."

"The truth is hard sometimes."

"Some truths are. But the one I'm talking about wasn't. It's beautiful, and I'm so happy I found it."

He looked confused.

She circled his neck with her arms. "I love you, Paul."

He stood stock-still a long moment. "You're sure?"

"Positive." She dipped her chin. "You're not going to run on me, are you? Because if you are, I'll tell you right now, I'll just hunt you down. I didn't get to be Lost, Inc.'s top investigator by quitting. I always find the lost."

"I'm not running." He smiled. "Della, you're the answer to my prayers."

He hadn't given her the words. Was that significant?

It wasn't. He'd shown her he loved her in thousands of ways—and with luck would thousands more. In his own time… in God's perfect time.

Dead by dawn.

She smiled. The only thing dead between them was doubt and fear.

Love endured and thrived.

"Della?"

She looked at Paul.

"I love you." His voice brimmed with emotion.

She cupped his beloved face in her hands. Her heart filled and overflowed with a joy so rich and pure it left her breathless. *Blessed. So blessed.* "Yes. Yes, you do."

"Remember that deal we made about the right woman?"

"Yes."

"I found her," he said. "I'm hoping she'll want to marry me, but if she doesn't, I'll be looking to you to step in for her. And this time, I'm not teasing."

Della smiled. "I have a feeling when things calm down that woman will be only too happy to marry you, Paul Mason."

"Well, now." He smiled and swung an arm over her shoulder. "I guess that lets you off the hook."

"I guess it does." Laughing, Della pecked a kiss to his cheek. "Unless I decide to keep you myself."

"Mmm." He paused at the top of the staircase and looked into her eyes. His twinkled. "That'd be…convenient."

"That was my thinking." They linked arms, walked down the stairs and out of the office.

Together they had survived the darkest night.

* * * * *

Don't miss CHRISTMAS COUNTDOWN,
the next installment of LOST, INC.,
*Vicki Hinze's new miniseries for Love Inspired Suspense,
On sale December 2012!*

Dear Reader,

I read a quote by Maltbie Davenport Babcock. It read: "Perfect sympathy cannot spring from the imagination. Only they who have suffered can really sympathize. I am sure you are saying, like the little child in the dark, 'Speak, Lord, for Thy servant heareth.'"

It stayed on my mind. At times, we all find ourselves in a dark hallway and we search and search but can't find a door or see light at the end of the hall to get to the light, to life. We're stuck in the dark, and we flounder. Sometimes we feel we deserve to be stuck in the dark, and sometimes we know we are victims but think if we weren't supposed to be there, then we wouldn't be. So we seek answers in the struggle. *Why me, Lord? Why this?*

When the struggle is one inflicted on us by another, it can still be hard not to feel responsible, and if that injury is inflicted on one we're responsible for... Well, we can feel we don't deserve anything good in our lives again. That's what happens to Della Jackson in *Survive the Night*. My heart ached for her in her loss but also in her attempts to come to terms with a future she didn't feel she deserved.

I had to write Della and Paul's story. I had to know how she discovered the power of God's grace. I was deeply touched by it, and I hope you will be, too.

Blessings,
Vicki Hinze

Questions for Discussion

1. Della feels responsible for an injury she didn't inflict because it was her duty to protect the victim. She couldn't, and as a result she feels she doesn't deserve happiness or even small things. She doesn't feel she deserves even comfort. Have you ever felt undeserving? As if good things were meant for others but not for you? How did you address those feelings? Did you blame God? Turn toward Him, or away from Him?

2. Paul fears getting close to anyone will put them in jeopardy. More than anything, he wants a family of his own—the family he was denied growing up. How do you feel your growing years impacted what you want as an adult? And have you had to forfeit what you want most for the greater good of another?

3. Della's husband blamed her for the death of their son, though she was in a war zone far away at the time of his death. Her husband abandoned her, and she lost everything that most mattered to her. We often hear of couples who suffer the loss of a child and end up divorced. Why do you think that happens? What can be done to prevent the breakup of the marriage, too?

4. Paul's parents were self-absorbed. They loved each other but made little room in their lives for their children. Paul took on the role of a parent to his younger sister, Maggie—so she would grow up knowing she was loved. Della wondered who had loved Paul, and discovered his uncle Warny discovered the way his parents treated Paul and Maggie and he became active in their lives. Do you think God compensates in such ways? Brings someone into our lives

to fill a role that needs filling? Is there an uncle Warny in your life? Do you fill that role in someone else's life?

5. A significant event happens to Della that changes her perspective and encourages her to open her heart spiritually and emotionally. After a traumatic event that forces a person to shut down, when that person reengages, as she does, do you think then that person is at peace with the past? Or do you think that bits and pieces of that past continue to influence them the rest of their lives? And is that influence constructive or destructive or both?

6. God gifted us with free will. So He can't intercede unless we ask. Asking is difficult for Paul and Della and for many of us. Was learning that God stands waiting, eager to be involved in the details of our lives a surprise? Or have you been aware of it all along?

7. Paul, through his work at Vet Net, tries to help returning soldiers reintegrate into civilian life. He tries to make a difference, to make the soldiers' lives better. That's very important to Paul, who felt insignificant most of his life because of his parents' treatment of him. Have you been around others who have made you feel insignificant? Have you made others feel insignificant? What did the firsthand experience teach you?

8. Della loved her husband and son unconditionally. When she lost them both, she was determined never to love again—her heart couldn't stand that kind of pain twice in a lifetime. And yet love finds its way into her heart, and it terrifies her. Have you felt vulnerable or afraid to love or to care too much? If so, how did you work through it? What was the result? What would you do the same? Do differently?

9. Through no fault of her own, Della had to start over with everything she never wanted. She felt so lost and alone, and deemed that she deserved to be alone, doomed to suffer. Have you ever experienced that kind of loss? That level of isolation? Did you overcome it? How? What role did your spiritual life play in that journey?

10. It is said that best friends make good partners, and yet one must ask, "What if the partnership fails? Then I've lost it *and* my best friend." That's the situation for both Paul and Della. The risks are high. Are they too high to pay? Would you risk losing your best and only true friend on a partnership that might or might not work? Why? Why not?

REQUEST YOUR FREE BOOKS!

2 FREE RIVETING INSPIRATIONAL NOVELS
PLUS 2 FREE MYSTERY GIFTS

Love Inspired®
SUSPENSE

Kathryn Springer

inspires with her tale of a soldier's promise
and his chance for love in

The Soldier's Newfound Family

When he returns to Texas from overseas, U.S. Marine
Carter Wallace makes good on a promise: to tell a fallen
soldier's wife that her husband loved her. But widowed
Savannah Blackmore, pregnant and alone, shares a different
story with Carter—one that tests everything he believes.
Now the marine who never needed anyone suddenly
needs Savannah. Will opening his heart be the
bravest thing he'll ever do?

—◄ TEXAS TWINS ►—

Available November 2012

www.LoveInspiredBooks.com

LI87776